Shadow of a Tiger

■ ■ ■

*#5 in the Edgar Award-winning
Dan Fortune Mystery series*

Dennis Lynds

Originally published under the pseudonym Michael Collins

Shadow of a Tiger e-book edition: 978-1-941517-08-6

Shadow of a Tiger POD edition: 978-1-941517-09-3

For inquiries:
Gayle Lynds
P.O. Box 732
125 Forest Avenue
Portland, ME 04101-9998
www.DennisLynds.com

*To Marie McErlean,
who is no pantywaist*

Acclaim for Dennis Lynds & His Novels

The New York Times named Shadow of a Tiger *one of the Year's Best Mysteries*

"First-class ... suspenseful, character-rich, and absorbing." – *Kirkus Reviews*

"Some of the rawest, most unencumbered mystery writing extant in the genre." – *American Library Association*

"Subtle undercurrents, handled with perception and realism ... a logical conclusion of force and stunning power." – *Utica Observer-Dispatch*

"[His novels are] filled with as much closely observed incident and detail as John O'Hara's short stories ..." – *Wall Street Journal*

"A master of crime fiction." – *Ellery Queen Mystery Magazine*

"Tough, believable." – *San Francisco Examiner*

"The man who won the Mystery Writers of America award ... has given readers another exceptional story." – *Parade of Books*

"Skillfully plotted with finely honed suspense." – *New York Times*

"[Lynds] is a writer to watch and above all to read." – Ross Macdonald

"Smashing ... leaves the reader breathless." – *Publishers Weekly*

"[He] carries on the Hammett-Chandler-Macdonald tradition with skill and finesse." – *Washington Post Book World*

"...combines superb characters and excellent plotting." – *ALA Booklist*

"... powerful writing." – *Library Journal*

"... engrossing and empathic." – *New York Daily News*

"... hot mystery writer whose novels have reached mainstream status. ..." – *San Diego Reporter*

"Collins is the Costa-Gavras of the PI world ... we might also call him the Captain Kirk of PI writers, boldly taking the genre where no colleague has gone before – and doing it so passionately that we can't help but sign on for the quest with him." – literary critic Francis M. Nevins, Jr.

"Lynds is a major contributor to the form, even a redefiner of it; whether or not he is ever given his just due, he should take satisfaction from the fact that he has written mystery novels of genuine distinction." – literary critic Richard Carpenter

Dan Fortune series, by Dennis Lynds, originally published under the pseudonym Michael Collins

> *Act of Fear*, 1967
> *The Brass Rainbow*, 1969
> *Night of the Toads*, 1970
> *Walk a Black Wind*, 1971
> *Shadow of a Tiger*, 1972
> *The Silent Scream*, 1973
> *Blue Death*, 1975
> *The Blood-Red Dream*, 1976
> *The Nightrunners*, 1978
> *The Slasher*, 1980
> *Freak*, 1983
> *Minnesota Strip*, 1987
> *Red Rosa*, 1988
> *A Dangerous Job*, 1989
> *Chasing Eights*, 1990
> *The Irishman's Horse*, 1991
> *Cassandra In Red*, 1992

Paul Shaw series, by Dennis Lynds, originally published under the pseudonym Mark Sadler

> *The Falling Man*, 1970
> *Here to Die*, 1971
> *Mirror Image*, 1972
> *Circle of Fire*, 1973
> *Touch of Death*, 1981
> *Deadly Innocents*, 1986

Kane Jackson series, by Dennis Lynds, originally published under the pseudonym William Arden

> *A Dark Power,* 1968
> *Deal in Violence*, 1969
> *The Goliath Scheme*, 1971

Die to a Distant Drum, 1972
Deadly Legacy, 1973

Buena Costa County series, by Dennis Lynds, originally published under the pseudonym John Crowe
Another Way to Die, 1972
A Touch of Darkness, 1972
Bloodwater, 1974
Crooked Shadows, 1975
When They Kill Your Wife, 1977
Close to Death, 1979

George Malcolm, private detective, by Dennis Lynds, originally published under the pseudonym Carl Dekker
Woman in Marble, 1973

Langford ("Ford") Morgan, ex-soldier, ex-CIA, ex-roustabout, by Dennis Lynds, originally published under the pseudonym Michael Collins
The Cadillac Cowboy, 1995

Other of his works include science fiction novels, literary novels, mystery short stories, literary short stories, short story anthologies, and poetry.

Table of Contents

1

You never see a Chinese drunk. Not in public. So I noticed the middle-aged Chinese man carrying his bottle in a paper bag down Ninth Avenue near Marais's pawn shop. Maybe I should have seen an omen, a break in the natural order of things, but I was thinking about Marty, and the ring I was taking to the pawn shop.

Marty is my girl—at my age, a woman. Martine Adair, who understands me. The ring was the only good present I'd ever given her. It had been to the pawn shop before, but this time I was uneasy about it. Because of this morning.

"I've got to get away, Dan," Marty said this morning. "Do something, anything. This awful heat."

It was the end of July, hot enough to melt brass, but it wasn't the heat on Marty's mind. Something else. I heard it in those words—"Do something, anything." Her show had just closed suddenly, she had no summer stock work. In three weeks the only work she had found was back taking off her clothes in one of the Third Street tourist clubs. She hadn't had to do that in over two years. I had to understand her, too.

"Fire Island?" I said. "Rent a house for a while?"

We were in her apartment on West Fourth Street, even the sheets on the bed limp from the heat. I knew how much she liked Fire Island, a house among the successful theater people.

"Yes!" she said, kissed me. "Sun and some peace."

"I couldn't even pay the ferry fare, Marty," I said.

She sat up in the bed beside me. She lit a cigarette.

"All right. Hock the damned ring."

"It's that important?" I said.

"Marais will give you five hundred for it. With that we can pay for a month. I won't go back to the G-string."

So it was just after five that evening, the tar melting on Ninth Avenue, that I was outside Marais's pawn shop and saw the Chinese drunk. The omen. Not that it would have made any difference in the end if I had sensed it was an omen.

Most stereotypes are true. The Chinese *don't* drink in public; the Irish *are* drinkers; the Germans do tend to arrogance; the English are conceited; the French do think a lot about women. The trouble is that they are general truths, none of them can be trusted in any single case. Eugene Marais, owner of the pawn shop, was French, but all Chelsea knew that Marais had never looked at another woman since he had married Viviane under the guns of the Germans in 1942, and Jimmy Sung was a drunk. Then, Jimmy Sung was more American than Chinese anyway. Chinese only in his silence and his smile.

They always smile, the Chinese in America. Maybe because they are few, and vulnerable, and a long way from home. Small people, and I don't mean in size. Small people you never really *saw*. Like Jimmy Sung. Night clerk, store clerk, odd-job man; an anonymous smile in the background. Except when he was drunk, the brown paper bag clutched in front of him the way it was now. No smile, his broad face and almond eyes unseeing under thin gray hair. The face of a man who sees a distant goal, is thinking of nothing else. His eyes glazed, his stocky body bent sideways on its crabwise course for home and the bottle.

I had my own troubles. I turned into Marais's pawn shop without looking at Jimmy Sung again. A tall man was coming out of the pawn shop. He was looking backwards into the shop. I stopped, he didn't. He bumped hard into me. He had weight and muscles. I grabbed him with my lone arm to keep from being knocked over.

"Ahhhhh!"

With the sharp, surprised cry, the tall man pulled back. As if my touch were contaminated. He brushed my hand away. His eyes were angry. Icy and belligerent. He was tall, imperious.

"Take care, please!"

It was a snapping rebuke, too strong. An excessive reaction startled out of him by bumping into me. A kind of reflex, like an old western hero reaching for his gun. Six-feet-two or more, he was ramrod straight as he looked down at me. An expensive, tailored dark blue jacket with pocket flaps, brass buttons, a suggestion of epaulets, and a shade too long for current fashion. Lighter blue slacks, a light blue shirt of heavier military cloth, and a blue and red regimental tie. Custom-made, the clothes, and a strong suggestion of a uniform. Some foreign uniform. A soldier temporarily out of wars, but military and assured, in command, stepping back and waiting for my salute.

I didn't salute. "Try looking where you're going!"

You—

The change was in his eyes, his whole manner. A flinch as if I'd slapped his face—as excessive as his first reaction in reverse. Quick, and then gone as fast as it had come. His smile back, the handsome face bending toward me in a return salute as if I had saluted. The hint of superiority and power, but controlled and courteous to inferiors.

"Pardon, then, of course. Stupid of me. My apology."

Smooth, the generous apology that somehow forgave *me*. Like the Archduke who stood aside to let the ill-mannered Beethoven pass. Proving that he, the Archduke, was the gentleman, and Beethoven the common slob. With his apology the tall man left me, somehow, in the wrong, and strode to the curb and a small, elegant foreign car. With a last smile, another faint bow of his handsome, blond head from the open car, he drove away, leaving no doubt who was the officer and gentleman.

The pawn shop bell tinkled as I closed the door and stood in the hot, cluttered shop with its locked grilles. No one was in the shop. The back room door was open. I walked to the rear, to where I could see into the back room.

Eugene Marais sat inside the room behind a battered table in his perpetual open-necked white shirt and baggy gray trousers. He wasn't alone. A short, broad man in a worn tweed jacket despite the heat stood talking to the pawn shop owner. They hadn't heard me, or, for some reason, the tinkle of the bell.

". . . he doesn't usually like to talk about Vel d'Hiv," the stocky stranger was saying. "He's not often that jumpy."

"You know Manet long, Claude?" Eugene Marais said.

"He was sent to me on business. I'm not interested."

"So?" Eugene Marais said. "Well, Paul Manet does not concern me, but you do, Claude. You are not interested in his business. What are you interested in, *hein?*"

"Very little, Eugene. Does that bother you so much?"

"When does the defeat end, Claude? When do you forget, decide that today is not yesterday? Settle, plan?"

"Everything is yesterday. For you too, Eugene."

"No," Eugene Marais said. "Everything is today. You are bad for my daughter, Claude. An empty man."

"Then I had better leave the city, yes?"

"I did not say that you had—"

In the shop I moved and made a noise. The two men didn't hear me, but the woman did. A woman who had been in the back room all the time, in full view, but who was so silent and immobile that I hadn't seen her. Like part of the room, a decoration on the walls. A tiny woman in a high-necked silk dress of pale blue brocade. An Oriental face, soft and childlike. Yet with the mature expression and bearing of an older woman. She heard me, stepped forward and touched the stocky stranger. Eugene Marais saw me through the doorway. He stood, smiled.

"Mr. Fortune? Is Jimmy not out there to serve you?"

"He's gone home," I said. "No hurry."

The pawn shop owner looked at his watch. "Ah, five-thirty already? Of course Jimmy has gone. I am so sorry."

Marais was a small man of fifty-two with a square, lined face and thick black hair. Above the open white shirt, his face was quiet and pleasant, with calm, light blue eyes. A man known to give the best deal on a pawn for ten blocks around. Only the perpetual cigarette, wet and loose in the center of his mouth, showed that he was not all calm inside.

"Family talk, one forgets time," Marais said. "You have not met my brother Claude. This is Mr. Daniel Fortune, Claude, a private detective." Marais smiled. "A hard policeman, as I am a ruthless money-lender, yes?"

"Mr. Fortune," the stocky Claude Marais said. The brother had a low, taciturn voice. His manner was distant, even with his brother, as if he weren't really in the room. "Is it interesting work, chasing the evildoer? Justice and retribution?"

"Mostly money and big dreams, Mr. Marais," I said.

"Always money, yes," the brother said. "Of course."

Eugene Marais said, "Claude forgets his manners. This lady is his wife, Li, Mr. Fortune."

I said, "Mrs. Marais."

Li Marais moved her delicate head in the faintest of bows. She withdrew again to the wall, silent. It was my day for stereotypes—a Caucasian can't guess the age of an Oriental. Maybe twenty-five, but I wasn't sure. I wasn't even sure what kind of Oriental she was—Chinese? Vietnamese? Burmese? No, thinner than a Burmese, and not Malaysian. She looked no more than twenty-five, yet she was very womanly, and Claude Marais had to be forty-five.

The brother walked past me. "Come, Li."

She followed him out through the shop. Her walk was a glide. So was Claude Marais's walk. As if he were a man trained to move lightly, but tired now, his heart not in the necessity to move anywhere. When they had both gone, Eugene Marais looked after them and sighed:

"He drifts, Claude. A sad thing."

"I never knew you even had a brother," I said.

He shrugged. "In eighteen years I have seen Claude three times. Only eight years between us, but what years. I am of the big war, the Occupation, the leaving of France. He was a child in the war, and he did not leave. The abyss between us. He became a hero to atone for my generation's defeat. Then it was his turn for defeat—Dienbienphu, Algeria. Now there is no France for him, and nowhere else. Ah, this stupid world!" The Gallic shrug again. "But you are here for money?"

I gave him the ring. "Marty needs a vacation."

He took the ring, unlocked his cash cage, went to the open safe. He had seen the ring before. He counted out five hundred dollars, pushed the bills through the grille to me.

"A vacation is better than diamonds," he said, smiled. "I and Viviane must take one. Jimmy guards my business better than I do. He thinks I am much too soft, do not drive the good bargain. Claude could help him while I was gone."

"It's better to be soft. You can live with it."

"Be the man who does nothing to anyone, eh? Sometimes even nothing can be too much. But you have your vacation to arrange, and I have work to do. *Bien*, eh?"

As I walked to Marty's apartment with the money, the night hadn't cooled a degree yet. Marty wasn't at home. She should have been there. To make our plans. Where was she? Call it a feeling, but this morning I had sensed something in her, a decision. A choice. She had to "do" something.

The heat on the crowded streets was like thick syrup. I wasn't hungry, but it was time to eat, so I stopped at the Acme Diner for the special roast beef.

The beef like a lump inside me, I called Marty. No answer. She knew I would have the money. So she wasn't anxious. My stomach was heavy from more than undigested roast beef. I was nervous about the five hundred, too. I walked across town to my one-room office on Twenty-eighth Street to lock the money up for the night.

My corridor was dim as usual, the single bulb over the stairs feeble in the stifling air. All the offices were dark, even the two old pornographers had left their treasures to try for some air somewhere. I decided on an air-conditioned movie as I unlocked my door.

The woman stepped out of the shadows of the corridor.

"Mr. Fortune?"

It was the tiny, Oriental wife of Claude Marais.

She sat in my one extra chair, her smooth face as clear as marble, her passive eyes like obsidian or black jade. I had thought her too small for me, too childlike and fragile. But close now, I saw that her body filled the pale blue dress in solid curves. Good curves—a woman.

"Eugene has said you are a detective?" she said.

"Yes." I was behind my desk, the money in a drawer.

"I would like to hire you, then."

They didn't look like they had money, she and the brother, but the straw floated through my mind to grasp at.

"I charge a hundred a day, one week minimum," I said. I didn't, not in Chelsea, but it was a try.

"I have only five hundred dollars," she said.

Her English was flawless, only a faint accent and that probably French. A difference mainly in the diction, foreign. I thought about her English to keep from feeling a louse. I needed that five hundred dollars.

"Fine," I said. I felt a louse. Talked to cover. "Where are you from, Mrs. Marais?"

"I am Thai. Siamese, perhaps you say."

Soft, young, yet that dignity that suggested experience if not age. A mature manner—Madame.

"What do you want to hire me to do?" I said.

"My husband was a soldier. Many years, many places. He has enemies. Now one wishes to kill him, I think. I do not know his name. Claude does not tell me what is in his mind, but I know he is in danger. Another soldier, I think, one I have seen before in Saigon, Bangkok, Hong Kong. Tall, perhaps forty. A German, with a limp and scars here." She touched her left cheek. "I have heard Claude speak on the telephone. This man comes to our hotel perhaps tonight, perhaps tomorrow. Claude is worried, I know that. He carries his pistol."

"One man? This German?"

"Perhaps there are others, I am not sure."

"What do you expect me to do?"

"Be at our hotel to stop this man before he comes to Claude. Do not tell Claude. I think that if this man sees that someone is watching Claude, he will go away. He, too, is an alien, such men are not fool-hardy. He will go."

"Such men as what, Mrs. Marais?"

"The men without countries, without simple work. The homeless men who live by their wits. He will go when he sees that Claude is not alone, that someone watches."

I didn't like the sound of it. She wanted someone there, but to do what, really? Scare this man? Why? Who was after whom? Did they need a demonstration of muscle, this woman and her husband, Claude? Or was it just her, some trick *against* the husband? But I watched her stand up now, lay five hundred dollars on my old desk, and what did I care what she really wanted? A risk? Maybe, but the money was there, and, somehow, I sensed that this time hocking a ring was not going to be good for me. This time, for Marty, I needed to have more to give. I picked up the money.

She said, "We are at the Stratford Hotel. It is on Ninth Street. Room 427. The man will come. You will tell him you watch Claude, send him away. Yes?"

"I'll be there," I said.

When she had gone I sat for a time. I didn't like it at all—but I had five hundred dollars. I could get the ring back. Maybe that would help.

2

I called Marty, there was still no answer. The pawn shop would be closed. There was nothing to do but the job I had been paid to do. I stopped for three cold cans of beer on the way, carried them with me.

The Hotel Stratford was middle class, not expensive but not a flop, either. The lobby was small but clean, the floor carpeted, and greenery in the pots. The heavy chairs and couches weren't too old. A solid hotel where they even cleaned the single elevator. The night clerk was just as solid, neither old nor young, neat and a friend.

"I'm going to wait for someone asking for room 427 or Claude Marais, George. I'll be quiet, and I'd appreciate a high sign. Okay?"

"Any trouble involved, Dan?" George Jenkins asked.

"Just talk, I hope. It's worth ten, okay?"

"Keep your money, Dan. Drink the beer out of sight, and put the cans in the bag. The manager's touchy."

I nodded thanks—ten saved is ten earned—and found an armchair where a rubber plant hid me. I could see the entrance, desk, elevator and stairs. There were no other ways up. The lobby wasn't air-conditioned, and the chair was heavy and hot. It was going to be a bad night.

For money and nothing else. I felt like a fool, a tool, or worse. A job I really knew nothing about, and didn't care a damn about—because I had to have money. Work I should have turned down because it was work in the dark, but a desperate man can't afford that luxury. The story of most men.

I had just finished my first beer when the stocky younger brother came out of the elevator and headed for the street. I had been paid to keep anyone away from Claude Marais, so I went out after him. In the stifling night, he turned uptown on Ninth Avenue. He didn't act like a man with someone out to kill him. He just walked uptown in that slow, gliding walk as if he had a weight dragging him back. When he crossed Nineteenth Street, I guessed where he was going.

There was a light inside the pawn shop of Eugene Marais as Claude turned into it. He had to wait for the door to be opened. After he had gone in, I took up a station across the street, lit a cigarette, and waited. The whole city was out in shirtsleeves, walking aimlessly in a vain attempt to find, or make, a breeze.

It was just past nine when Claude Marais came out of the pawn shop again. He wasn't alone. A short young girl was with him—heavy-bodied and big-breasted, her dark hair long on her bare shoulders, her face full-lipped and petulant. She wore a loose blouse off her shoulders, and tight shorts, and I recognized her—Danielle Marais, Eugene's daughter. Nineteen, her heavy body was full and sensual.

I followed them back to the Stratford. They went up together. I wondered if the wife, Li, was up in the room? After all, what did I really know about why I had been hired? Or who I was really staked out to watch for?

Somewhere around ten, a big puff of cooler air ran around the lobby for a time, and I finished my second beer. I was about to open the third before it boiled, and almost missed the night clerk's high sign.

The youth at the desk wasn't middle-aged, scarred or German, but he had asked for Claude Marais or his room, and I cornered him at the elevator. I knew him—a twenty-year-old street kid from south of Houston Street: Charlie Burgos.

"Visiting friends, Charlie?"

He curled his lip. "What's it to you, Fortune?"

Defensive and aggressive—both together, and immediately. Defensive, because like all street kids of the slums he knew his powerlessness. Aggressive, because aggression, immediate and animal, was the only hope of power any street kid had. Strike before you're struck. The street kids of poor, dirty, tough, abandoned streets that didn't exist to the daylight world of affluent America.

"I'm going to check you out, Charlie," I said.

He had been checked for weapons all his young life, Charlie Burgos, whenever he ventured beyond his own streets and alleys. Guilty, until reluctantly found innocent by cops who knew that crime *did* live in the slums.

"Check," Charlie Burgos said, indifferent.

My right to check him was power, nothing more. Physical power because I was older, social power because I had at least some standing in the proper community. Not like Charlie Burgos or his parents—they had no power, so no rights. Parents who had never escaped the same streets—uneducated, unskilled, without hope of a human joy beyond the bottle, the needle, the bookie, the street woman, and some joyless job with nowhere to go except down. No today, no tomorrow, beyond what they could steal, for a moment, from each other's flesh.

He had no weapon. "Okay, Charlie. What's up?"

He showed no resentment to being searched. Abstract anger and pride was a luxury street kids don't have. Kids put down and ignored forever because they were young, and poor, and powerless. Lost to disease and drugs, but lost mostly to defeat. There are few fair ways out of the defeat of the slums, so they learn early to lie, cheat, steal, mug and scheme every minute. An angle, a scheme of profit, that is what they live with, and that was what was on Charlie Burgos's mind.

"You on a job, Fortune? Stake out? Buck an hour, I'll help, okay?"

"What's your business with Claude Marais, Charlie?"

"Nothin'. It's hot, take a break. I'll spell you."

"Never mind, Charlie."

"I'll go for a beer. Buck for goin' to the store."

I went back to my chair behind the rubber plant. The third beer was hot, damn! At the elevator, Charlie Burgos was gone. The wife, Li Marais, had said others might be involved, but Charlie wasn't armed, and if he had anything on his mind he wasn't going to tell me without more pressure.

I got my answer anyway. At ten-forty, my last beer gone, Charlie Burgos came out of the elevator—with Danielle Marais. The ripe pawn-shop owner's daughter held the tall, skinny street kid's arm. In his dark-eyed animal way, Charlie Burgos was handsome enough. He gave me a wink as they passed—"Look what I'm going to get, mister. I howl tonight!" the wink said. It's the only relation to a woman a street kid knows.

He came into the lobby at 11:02 P.M. Taller than I had expected, the limp barely noticeable, but the scars clear on his left cheek.

He walked straight through the lobby to the desk, seemed to look at nothing and no one. Yet he saw everything and everyone. He seemed to look straight ahead, intent on where he was going, yet I saw his eyes on me. German eyes under thin blond hair—pale blue, smooth, self-contained.

Forty-plus, I guessed, but the stride of an athlete in shape. Not furtive, but calling no attention, either. Polite and reserved in a brown tropical suit he wasn't quite at home in. He wore the suit casually, but somehow seemed restricted by it. He belonged in safari clothes in some jungle, or running guns in a fast boat. The kind of man who would sell both sides if he could, and would be wanted in many countries for a little official talk. A man who would live high, hard and well, until he ended in front of a firing squad in some remote capital, or, worse, slowly ran out of countries where he could go, people he could live off.

The clerk gave me the high sign, but I was already on my way to the elevator. When he came, I was in his path. I could see the gun under his right arm. He stopped. Surprised to see me in his path, but not scared.

"You're looking for Claude Marais?" I said.

He thought about it. "Yes, I visit Claude."

"For what reason?"

He thought about me. He considered my one arm. I sounded tough, and he had no way of knowing if I was or wasn't.

"It is your affair?"

"It is now," I said, and flashed an old private guard badge.

His blond eyebrows went up an inch. He looked at my arm.

"Special detective," I said, before he could ask about a cop with one arm. "You're an alien, you have a permit for that gun you're carrying?"

His left hand moved to his thin blond hair, combed through. A mannerism. I imagined him doing that when deciding if he should shoot a prisoner or not.

"Claude, he is in some trouble?" he said.

"Let's say I'm watching him. I want to know your business."

"A private matter. Personal. I wish no trouble."

"Good," I said. "Maybe I better take the gun."

I held out my hand, and he reacted. Like a snake. He jerked back, took two steps away. I could see him thinking. Somehow, though, he wasn't acting like a man out to kill anyone. More like a man with a plan on his mind, weighing how important it was that he see Claude Marais. He decided.

"I wish no trouble," he said again as if his mind could hold only limited thoughts in English. "Claude is not important to me that much. *Bitte.*"

He backed away, didn't turn until he was past the desk. Then he strode out of the lobby. I wiped the sweat from my face. Killer or not, he was a man I wouldn't want to cross where he had the advantage. I followed him out. Across the street I saw him climb into a blue Ford and drive away.

I waited an hour hidden outside the hotel entrance. The German didn't return. I had a pretty good certainty that he wouldn't, not tonight, at least. It was twelve-ten, I had done my job, and I was tired. I went home to bed.

I didn't sleep much, not in the oven of my five shabby rooms. Not until just before dawn when a faint coolness seemed to wash in through the open windows. A gray dawn light, cooler . . .

13

Then he was there. He had a gun.

"Who are you, Mr. Fortune?" he said, a shape beside my bed in the dawn. "What do you want with me? With Exner?"

I rolled onto my back under the sheet, blinked at him. He stood over the bed: Claude Marais.

"How'd you get in here, Marais?" I said.

He waved the pistol. I was changing the subject. "A man learns to open doors. I want to know who you really are, what you were doing at my hotel last night?"

His pistol was steady—an odd pistol. An unusually long barrel for a light gun—7.65-mm. A French Starr.

"Can I get a cigarette?" I said.

He hesitated. I realized that my empty sleeve was hidden under the sheet. Last night he hadn't even noticed I had only one arm. A man busy with his own thoughts.

"I've only got one arm," I said, showed him.

"All right, get a cigarette," he said. "A war injury?"

"No." I smoked. "You know who I am. Your brother—"

"My brother said you are a detective. That doesn't tell me of your past, of who you work for, or why you are mixed in my affairs. It doesn't tell me why you were waiting for Gerd Exner, or how you knew Exner was coming to me last night."

"Why was Exner coming to you?" I said.

"My business," Claude snapped. "Did my brother send you?"

"Eugene? Why would Eugene send me? Does he know—"

"Do not answer me with questions, Fortune. Gerd Exner says you claimed to be a policeman. That has alarmed him. Why did you scare him? For whom? What did you think you were doing?"

"Why does Exner want to kill you, Claude?"

"Kill me?" The surprise was genuine. Damn the woman.

"Your wife said Exner wanted to kill you."

"My wife?" He stopped. "Ah, I see. Yes." He lowered the pistol. "I have not given her very much. No home, no life, no rest. I understand now. Has she paid you?"

"Yes." Too much. I hoped he wouldn't ask.

He pocketed the pistol. "All right, but I am in no danger. My wife made a mistake. I will explain to her. Finished, yes?"

He walked out. I lay back. I was home free. No more job, and I kept the money. I had some curiosity about Claude Marais and the German, but not enough to think about it very hard.

I decided to surprise Marty with the ring. I went out and ate a slow breakfast, and then walked to the pawn shop. It was open. Inside, I saw Eugene Marais sitting in the back room.

"Dig out my ring, Marais," I said. "I got lucky."

Then I saw the chessmen. A bishop, two pawns, and a knight on the floor in the back room doorway. I went into the back room. Eugene Marais was tied to his chair by a single strand of rope. Blood had trickled from his nose and right ear—black, dried blood. The crusted wound was on the back of his head. He had been hit hard once. I felt him. He was rigid as steel.

Dead at least four hours, at most twelve. Probably somewhere in between.

3

By 11:00 A.M. it was ninety-two on Ninth Avenue, and Lieutenant Marx had rounded up Claude Marais and his wife, Li; the dead pawn shop owner's daughter Danielle; and Jimmy Sung. One of Marx's men had been sent to Brooklyn for Eugene Marais's wife, the others had been going over the shop for two hours.

The shop had been half ransacked—parts a jumble of debris, other parts not touched. As if someone had made a selective search—looking for something specific—or as if the job had been only half done. The cash drawer inside the broken cage was on the floor, but some three hundred dollars had been left, overlooked, and the safe hadn't been opened. A chess board was set up on the table, but the men had been scattered. The rope bound the dead man to the chair by only the one strand, as if the killer had realized he didn't have to tie the dead man after all.

I said, "He didn't know Marais was dead at first."

"Maybe, Dan," Lieutenant Marx said.

The assistant Medical Examiner talked as he washed his hands. A small, neat, nervous doctor.

"Complete rigor. So four to twelve hours, except that in this heat it gets speeded up. From other signs, I'd say anywhere from five this morning, to eleven last night. Maybe earlier, maybe later, but I'd have to doubt it in court. The autopsy may give us a closer guess."

"What killed him, Doc?" Marx said.

"Fractured skull, pieces in the brain. That iron rod on the floor has blood on it. One blow. I'll tell you in detail after autopsy, but it looks simple to me."

"Hit from behind," Marx decided. "In this room, from that blood near the door. Any prints on the iron bar?"

"Nothing we could identify," a detective said.

The M.E. signaled his men to put Eugene Marais into the morgue basket. For an instant everything stopped, all silent, as if the world was standing still. We all looked at the body and the basket. Then it was gone, and we all began to move. Life and work goes on, death forgotten after that one instant because it has to be.

The daughter, Danielle, looked at the basket as it went out, but her eyes were stiff, unseeing. It was the only time she had looked at her father since the police had brought her in. Her eyes dull, without tears, where she stood out in the shop out of sight of the body. Her whole young, ripe body oddly stiff in the same blouse and shorts she had worn last night. Her surly, adolescent face closed up like someone who waited for a blow.

Claude Marais had stood over the body since the moment he had arrived, his hand touching his dead brother as if to offer comfort, to sustain the dead man. He watched us all with a bruised, baleful glance. Intense and defiant, angry with death. Yet behind his eyes there was something like a question, as if he were trying to understand something only he knew.

"What did he do? Eugene?" the stocky brother had said to everyone and to no one, to the ransacked shop itself. "Nothing. He used to say that himself. He had done nothing, hurt no one, helped no one. No enemies, no comrades. Never accused, never honored. He never risked, and he's dead anyway. Stupid!"

The brother hunched over as if cold even in his tweed jacket and heavy trousers in the heat. Cold while we all sweated, like a man who lived with a perpetual chill, an icy wind blowing always through his mind. He watched the morgue basket go out not with sorrow, but with a kind of rage.

His wife, Li Marais, sat silent in a corner, as still as a stone cat from some Egyptian tomb, only her onyx eyes alive. Cat eyes, bright and fixed. Looking at no one, and everyone.

Under the single, barred, back room window, Jimmy Sung squatted on his heels. The inscrutable Oriental—with a very American cigarette dangling from his full lips, and a very American scowl. The watery red eyes of the drunk, annoyed at being bothered on the morning after. He had said nothing since being brought to the shop, sure, like all alcoholics, that if he kept quiet he would look normal, and his secret would be hidden from everyone.

While Marx's men went on working over the shop, the Lieutenant began to question them all about the time element. After a few moments I stopped listening—none of them could really prove where they had been for most of the night. That was normal, so I let their voices fade to a drone in my mind, and began to check all the windows and the two doors. I studied the odd way the shop had been searched—almost at random.

I was still thinking about the search, when Marx told us all to come to the precinct station with him.

In the Lieutenant's cubicle command office off the squad room, I told him my story again. In murder, I don't often hold back from the police. It doesn't pay in the long run. Then Marx took them one at a time. Jimmy Sung was first.

The gray-haired Chinese shrugged. "I don't know nothing about Mr. Marais. I work in the shop six months—noon to five. We get along fine, ask anyone. Some punk robber, I figure."

He had no accent. Only an odd order of words showed that English had not been his first language. The words were pure American, a colloquial slum vocabulary; the manner flip, direct.

"You left about five last night?"

"Sure. Fortune saw me."

"You didn't go back to the shop?"

"Noon to five, that's all I work."

"Did Mr. Marais stay late often?"

"Not on your life. He ran home fast to Brooklyn."

"Why did he stay last night?"

"Who knows, Lieutenant?"

"You can't tell us anything, Jimmy?"

Jimmy Sung shrugged. "I think he got something on his mind, he don't tell me what. Five o'clock, I go home."

I said, "You play chess, Jimmy?"

His watery eyes looked at me, solemn. "Sometimes. Not last night, no sir."

Claude Marais still looked cold in his heavy jacket. His wife, Li, still looked like a small, silent cat in her chair that faced Marx behind his littered desk.

"What was bothering your brother, Mr. Marais?" Marx said.

"Nothing that I know," Claude Marais said.

I said, "What about that Gerd Exner? You seemed to think that Eugene might have hired me to stop Exner reaching you."

"Who else would be interested in my affairs? A mistake."

"You came back to the shop about eight-thirty last night?" Marx said.

"Eugene called me. Plans for a family weekend."

"He called you?" Marx said. "Why was he at the store?"

"I don't know."

"Why did your wife hire Fortune? Who is Gerd Exner?"

"An old business associate."

"What business?"

"Buying and selling." Claude Marais shrugged. "Trading, you see? Mostly in the Orient and Africa. It is past for me."

"You usually carry guns? You and your associates?"

"I have not lived in a peaceful world, Lieutenant. Mostly remote areas, unsettled countries. I have a valid permit."

"Why did your wife hire Fortune to stop this Exner?"

"A misunderstanding. She thought I was afraid of Exner. A simple error, that is all."

Li Marais said nothing, but she gave a slow nod as if to agree. I wasn't sure I believed the nod.

I said, "You play chess, Claude?"

"I never learned peaceful games."

"Was the chess game set up when you were there at nine?"

Claude thought. "I think it was. It often was."

"It wasn't when I was there about five," I said.

Lieutenant Marx said, "You left your brother alive about nine o'clock, Marais. You went back to your hotel with Danielle. About six A.M. you were in Fortune's apartment. Where were you in between those times?"

"In my room with my wife," Claude Marais said.

"Anyone who can prove that?"

"Only my wife."

Marx didn't even bother to ask Li Marais.

Danielle Marais didn't sit down. The heavy girl stood defiant in front of Lieutenant Marx's desk, glared at me, her oversize breasts like jelly under the tight blouse.

"I went to my father's store to borrow some money, that's all. I don't know why my father was working late. I left with Uncle Claude. My boy friend picked me up at Uncle Claude's hotel. We were together all night. I never saw my dad again. I don't know anything. Nothing!"

The words poured out, a torrent. Ready, as if she had a tape recording in her mind she only had to turn on. Memorized, defensive, defying before Marx had attacked.

"Did you get the money?" Marx said dryly.

"What?" she said, deflated. "No. He didn't have it."

"Your boy friend is Charlie Burgos?"

She nodded. "We went to his pad. We were there all night. You know that, your men picked me up there."

"But not Charlie. He wasn't there, was he? You're sure he was with you all night, and you never went home?"

"I'm not a kid," the girl said scornfully. "And Charlie was with me all night—in bed! You can't say he wasn't!"

"I didn't try—yet," Marx said.

She bit her full lips, glared at the Lieutenant like a child caught in some crime and rebuked.

Marx said, "Did Charlie have a key to the pawn shop? Your key, maybe?"

"You're crazy! I don't have a key!"

I said, "Charlie's a punk, Danielle, a schemer. Not his fault, maybe, but he'll drag you down. He's too smart to sink into the slums, but not smart enough to get out a straight way."

"Charlie's smarter than any of you!" Danielle said hotly. "He's going places, big places, and I'm going with him!"

"Why, Danielle?" I said. "You're no street kid. You have a good home, plenty of chances. You don't belong in the slums."

"You and my parents! I love Charlie, you hear? He's a real man. He's not a fat nothing who can't even make money out of a pawn shop!"

"What can Charlie make money out of?" Marx snapped.

"Anything!" she sneered. "Charlie's a leader."

"A leader in a cheap sewer, Danielle," I said. "You weren't surprised to find your father dead, were you? I think you knew he was dead before the police came. Was it an accident, Danielle? Charlie Burgos was robbing the store, and—"

"Charlie was in bed with me! All night! You can't make me say anything else! Some dumb robber, that's all! Or maybe ask Uncle Claude! He was supposed to go back to the shop. I heard my father tell him to come back!"

Claude Marais said, "I didn't go back. Eugene called it off."

"I don't suppose you can prove it?" Marx said.

"The hotel switchboard took a call for me from Eugene around eleven. Maybe they listened."

"It wouldn't prove anything anyway, would it?" Marx said. "You could have gone back anyway."

"I could have," Claude Marais agreed. "But I didn't."

I sat with Marx in his office. "What do you think?"

"Robbery," Marx said, "what else? Pawn shop. A prime target for small-timers, junkies, street kids."

"Three hundred in cash left? The safe not touched?"

"Panic. Points even more to junkies or kids."

"Maybe," I said. "What was actually taken?"

"We're still checking. Marais kept lousy records. Jimmy Sung and the wife, Viviane, are helping us check."

"Does the wife have an alibi?"

Marx sighed. "She was home all night—alone."

"So no one has an alibi. Jimmy Sung was curled up alone with his bottle. When I tailed the brother to the shop, he had to knock. The door was locked. I checked all doors and windows. No marks of entry, and most windows barred. Either the killer had a key, or Eugene Marais let him in. Which makes it an inside job. But then more should have been taken. With Eugene Marais dead, the killer had plenty of time."

"Except that he panicked when he saw Marais was dead."

"If he panicked, he wouldn't have stopped to search."

"Unless he hit Marais, started his search, decided to tie Marais up halfway, found him dead, and then ran."

Marx had a good point. I could see some thief hit Eugene Marais, start to ransack the shop, maybe hear a groan or just realize Marais might come awake, go back to tie the owner up, find him dead, and panic. That would explain the half search.

"I still don't like the entry," I said.

"All right, so maybe Marais left the door open by mistake later," Marx said. "It's too sloppy for an inside job. I figure an open door, a small-time thief. We'll find the loot, talk to our stoolies, and we'll have our killer."

"Maybe you will," I said, and I stood up. "Can I go to the shop and get my ring out of hock?"

"No, not until we inventory and release the stock."

4

I went to my one-window office and tried to call Marty again. No luck, so I spent the afternoon alone in the office, sweating and paying some bills, and hoping the telephone would and wouldn't ring. I wanted Marty to call me, but if the phone rang it might be Li Marais asking for some of her money back.

The phone did ring—twice. It wasn't Marty, or Li Marais, either time. The first call was a woman who wanted her fifteen-year-old daughter tailed, the second was a man who suspected his wife's nephew of stealing from his store. I turned down both jobs. I didn't like them, and I had five hundred dollars.

It was after 7:00 P.M when I finally found Marty at home. She told me to come over.

As I walked downtown in the hot evening, I suddenly felt like a boy really wanting a woman for the first time, nervous and afraid she wouldn't want him. Uncertain and shy, like a stranger to Marty, an unseen wall up between us.

The wall was there in her eyes as she opened her door and walked ahead of me into her living room. She repairs and refinishes all her own furniture. Antiques and junk, whatever meets her fancy. She works hard on it, a small woman in jeans and a stained man's shirt. Now she was a different woman—somehow taller, reserved in a slim green pants suit that had cost her three hundred dollars. She usually wore it only for business, for the theater. Not for me.

"I got the money," I said.

"That's fine," she said, sat on the long old couch I'd known for so many years now.

"I hocked the ring, but I got a job, too," I said. I didn't sit with her on the couch. I took a chair. "So I can get the ring back, okay? Where'll we go? Fair Harbor?"

"It's the best," Marty said.

"I'd have the ring back now, but the police are holding it. Eugene Marais was murdered in his store last night."

"No, Dan! Marais?" Her eyes widened, and narrowed with a kind of pain. "Who? Why? He was such a . . . kind man. My God, half the people we know hung on because Marais paid too much, bought what he couldn't really sell."

"A thief, it looks like. You know how pawn shops get hit."

"That's horrible." She was silent. "He asked so little for himself. Chance, Dan? Just stupid, blind chance?"

"I suppose so," I said. "It's all chance, Marty, all just accident. The good and the bad."

Her face went hard. "No, I can't believe that. A person has to make life happen, act to have what he wants. Good or bad, you have to have the life you decide you want."

"Meaning?" I said.

She didn't answer. She found a cigarette, lit it, her small face closed. Not a beautiful face, but pretty enough, and very alive.

I said, "I'm not sure Marais's murder was an accident. A lot's wrong. Call it a feeling, a theory. My hound nose."

"Theory?" she said. "Are you going to investigate?"

"No one's asked me."

"When did that stop you, Dan?" Marty said. "The observer, the detached theorizer. Curiosity and the hunt. The interesting puzzle. So neutral, Dan?"

I said, "What's wrong, Marty?"

She smoked in the hot living room. I waited, and out in the streets of the city twilight was turning to darkness. That sudden surge and fading of noise that comes in the city just at twilight.

"I'm not sure, Dan," she said.

"When will you be sure?"

She was silent again. "Dan? Don't plan Fire Island just yet. I'm not sure I want to do it that way. May be I want to be alone for a while."

"All right. Take my money. I'll get the ring when—"

"No, give me the pawn money," she said. "I have to think. I want to think, Dan. I can't live and die like Eugene Marais. What did he have? What did he do? Nothing."

"He had peace. Acceptance of what he was, and what the world is. And maybe his death wasn't blind chance."

"That's not enough for me. Not for any woman."

"Maybe not," I said.

I gave her the five hundred for the ring. She sat silent. I didn't want to leave then, but I left. A man is what he is.

I wanted to stay with Marty, show her that she was mine, make her want to be mine. I wanted to do that, but I never would. That doesn't make me much of a man, I know, but it makes me what I am. She had to shape her own life. All I could do was hope she would, in the end, want me. You owe every human being understanding, respect for their needs and wants. But that doesn't mean that you will like the results. To accept, understand, another person's needs, doesn't change one iota of what you need yourself.

I wanted to stay, but I left. Not much man. Not very strong. But a human being. At least, I like to think that's what I am. Sometimes I wonder even about that. The observer, even of myself.

So busy observing myself as I cut through the alley behind my five cheap rooms, that I never saw them until they had me trapped cold in the alley.

Four shadows. Two at each end of the dark alley.

Silent, they stood there.

Four quick, alert shapes that appeared to block my way front and rear. Coming up from nowhere, silhouetted against the feeble street light at either end of the alley in the hot night. Each a distinct shadow, a person, yet all the same—thin and without faces. They made no sound or movement, looming like thin birds of prey in the night.

I looked around the alley. Windowless walls on both sides, locked rear doors. No way out except past them. Nothing to help me except three ranks of garbage cans, and two cats that ran silently away as the four shadows began to move toward me.

They came bent forward, watching me warily like hunters approaching some cornered animal. An animal they weren't going to let escape, yet respected, so advanced carefully.

I didn't try to talk to them. They hadn't come to talk, at least not until they had given me their message in a more direct way.

I sidled toward a rank of six garbage cans.

The first attack came from behind me.

One jumped in alone, something in his raised right hand. A darting attack like a snake striking. Maybe he thought I was momentarily not looking behind me. Whatever, it gave me a faint chance. For a moment, he was alone.

It was a tire iron in his hand. I grabbed at his arm, missed, ducked under and in, took a hard blow from the tire iron on my left shoulder, and hit him in the belly.

A scrawny belly, my fist sinking almost to his backbone. He vanished, the tire iron clattering down on the cobblestones.

A shadow behind me.

I kicked over a garbage can, and the shadow sprawled and rattled among the cans.

Something like a club smashed against my nose and cheek. I tasted blood.

My hand closed on a thin, bony wrist. My face was close against a pale, hard-breathing face—a young face, with acne.

Kids!

Street kids. Thin, savage, crazy-eyed, breathing hard and silent as they swarmed over me as deadly as wild animals in any jungle.

I kicked the one I held. He fell away. I had a garbage can cover. I smashed it into a face. A long iron bar cracked my ribs. Something battered my head, my arm. They breathed, grunted, said nothing. They had not come to talk at all. To at least put me into some hospital.

I was bruised and bleeding—one arm against eight arms with weapons. But they were kids. There is a difference between a kid and an adult, even a street kid. It's called viciousness, the ability to attack totally without flinching. An adult has learned to hold back nothing in a fight. Most kids, if they are sane, sober and not on drugs, will hesitate a hair, flinch unsure, and that was what saved me.

That, and the fact that street kids are all muscle, but the muscles are starved. They are not in good shape or health. Pound for pound, they are weak compared to a well-fed, athletic suburban boy.

They had me, but they flinched. They could grab me, but they couldn't hold me.

I sank teeth into a face. I kicked bellies and groins. I stamped thin arms on the ground. I hammered them with my garbage can cover. I tangled them among the cans.

I saw a clear space, and ran. Unsure, without stamina, they gave me space and too much time, and I ran for the escape of the street. My street.

I saw them behind me. Two of them. The other two must have taken more from me than they could handle. I didn't know the two behind me, not exactly. Familiar faces, but I could fit no names to the faces.

I reached my building, locked the vestibule door, made it up the stairs to my five hot but secure rooms. In the room I waited. They didn't come up. It was my territory.

Shaking, I got to my bathroom. The mirror showed me cuts, blood and bruises. My ribs stabbed. My arm was limp, ached. I washed, daubed Merthiolate. My left eye was blackening, but I didn't think anything was broken. I sat down in my shabby living room in the hot night, lit a cigarette.

I hadn't recognized any of them, but I didn't have to. Street kids, they could have been sent by only one person—Charlie Burgos. A favor for Charlie, or maybe orders. Charlie himself hadn't been there, he was a leader. Besides, I would have recognized him. They had wanted at least to put me into the hospital. Why?

Eugene Marais's murder? Sure. But I wasn't really involved in that, was I? Another mistake like Li Marais hiring me to stop Gerd Exner? Or was Charlie Burgos showing off his power for Danielle Marais? I had bothered Danielle.

Maybe. Maybe this, and maybe that, and to hell with it. I hurt, I hadn't slept much last night, and I didn't give a damn about Charlie Burgos.

I went to bed.

To hell with Marty.

I went to sleep wondering what Charlie Burgos thought I was doing that I wasn't. To hell with it. But my mind wouldn't quit. The human problem—that damned mind of ours.

I awoke to the telephone ringing. It was my answering service. A Viviane Marais had called me about five last night. She wanted to see me.

5

Eugene Marais had lived in Brooklyn, out in Sheepshead Bay.

New York is a city of "villages," a series of neighborhoods each with its local life and natives. In these villages there are some who are important to the natives, but who are never really natives themselves—the white shopkeepers of Harlem who live in Queens; the black police captains who rule Bedford-Stuyvesant, but live in New Rochelle. Eugene Marais had been a fixture in Chelsea, but he had lived in Sheepshead Bay.

I took the subway. It was a trip into the past. When I was a boy in Chelsea, Sheepshead Bay was where we had gone fishing. An outing, an adventure; the clean air and the sea. Before I lost my arm and wandered far from Chelsea. Still, I remembered, and the smells of fish and sea came to greet me when I left the subway in the hot sun. But the Bay wasn't the same anymore.

When I was a boy it had been a fishing village—wooden piers, shops and restaurants on pilings over the water, Italian trawlers tied up drying their nets, hordes of gulls wheeling over the fish refuse dropped into the Bay. Now it was just another part of the city, the Belt Parkway knifing through it. Mayor LaGuardia had started the change; banning the trawlers, making the piers concrete, closing the shops over the water, cleaning it all up. A loss, a tragedy, yet the mayor could do nothing else. The city had been growing too fast. A small population can live casually with nature, its pollution swallowed up. A large one can't. Too many people must regulate how they live with nature, or destroy nature and themselves. So a fishing village was lost.

But not quite. I found Eugene Marais's house in a quiet old section not far from the water. Narrow old frame houses with porches and high attic windows. Trees and grape arbors. Out of time—as Eugene Marais himself had been, in a way. I went through the small yard of lawn and hydrangea bushes to the front door. Viviane Marais let me in herself.

She was a small, dark woman of fifty, with an energetic walk as she led me into an old-fashioned living room of delicate furniture, china bric-a-brac, and lace—very French. There was nothing old-fashioned about Viviane Marais. She wore a chic black sheath on a full yet firm figure that could handle it. She wore no jewelry, her fine features and erect carriage needing no adornment. Her eyes were dark and quick as she gave me a chair.

"Eugene spoke of you, Mr. Fortune. He liked you. Now I think I want to hire you."

"I liked him," I said.

She didn't sit. She lit a cigarette, French and masculine.

"Do you believe it was robbery, Mr. Fortune?"

"I'm not sure. Yes and no."

"I am sure, and it is no."

Small and determined, she began to pace with a dynamism Eugene Marais had lacked. A quiet, slowish man, and a fiery, energetic wife. Complementary? A good marriage?

"First," she said, smoked, "I think something had disturbed Eugene lately. I am not sure, he was not a man to trouble me with his worries, but I feel it now. Second, Eugene would not have resisted a thief. Money was not so important to him."

"He was hit from behind," I said.

She ignored that. "Too little was stolen, almost nothing of real value. Some cheap rings, some watches, useless objects. I have the police list."

She gave me the list. I read it. She was right—nothing but a seemingly random grab bag of cheap items, bric-a-brac.

She paced. "In a way, the shop was a charity. Eugene's idea of how to help small people. He said a pawn shop could help those no one else would—the drunkards, phonies, gamblers; the desperate and the forgotten."

She looked at me. "We have family money. The shop had to make us only a small income. Our needs were few: this house, food, an occasional night out. We have only Danielle."

She thought. "Eugene wanted no more children in this world. He said we could help those who were here, not bring more to suffer. He had little faith in values. From the past."

"What about the past?" I said. "A killer? A motive?"

"I can think of nothing," she said, paced. "Eugene never acted to hurt anyone. He never fought, had no politics. He did nothing much in this world, Mr. Fortune. A quiet man."

"A man who has done nothing to anyone," I said. "Eugene said that to me the night he was killed. Claude said something like it—no enemies, no comrades. Now you say just about the same. Coincidence, Mrs. Marais?"

For a time she was silent. Then she sat down facing me. She lit another cigarette. "Perhaps not. The words seem to be in my mind. I was thinking why that would be. It was Eugene, something he said. A small remark. While reading his newspaper one night, I think, perhaps a week ago. I took little notice, a husband and wife of thirty years, you know? But now?"

"What did he say?"

"That a man can spend his life doing nothing and harming no one, neither monster nor hero, and still there will be reasons for some to want him gone, nonexistent." She nodded to herself. "Yes, so the thought is in my mind. Perhaps he said much the same to Claude. In all our minds."

"You don't know what he might have meant?"

"No."

"Nothing special happened recently? Anything unusual?"

"Not that I know." She blew smoke in the room. "We lived a routine life, Mr. Fortune. Here at home. We read, walk, talk, make love. A quiet life, very good. Our only outside life is my church work and Eugene's Balzac Union—a French cultural club in New York he attended quite often at lunch, sometimes in the evening. Perhaps we lived so because we began in such chaos. The war, the Occupation, the Liberation. We were married in 1942 under German guns, German sneers, their arrogant eyes and boots everywhere. Eugene's older brother died in the war, my brother vanished in the Occupation, a gendarme cousin was killed by the Maquis, my parents died under your bombs in the Liberation. Chaos and destruction. Is it a wonder we wanted only private quiet?"

I said, "Eugene hadn't seen his brother in a long time, had he? When did Claude come to New York?"

"A few months ago. You can't think that Claude—!"

"What do you know about him? His life since Algeria? He's a closed-up, detached man. He says he worked in remote places where he needed a gun. He's got some peculiar friends. I heard Eugene say he was a drifter, a bad influence."

"On Danielle, we thought. But I doubt that anyone can be a worse influence on Danielle than her present friends," Viviane Marais said. "I am not sure exactly what Claude has done since he left the French army. A mercenary soldier, a pilot, a trader and guard for other traders. What else does he know to do? He was a bitter boy against we who lost to the Germans. He had to defend the honor and glory of France. Eugene had not a high opinion of the honor and glory of France, or of any nation or people. They argued in the old days, saw little of each other over the years. A few months ago Claude appeared here with his wife, moved into that hotel, has done very little since."

"Waiting?" I said. "For someone or something?"

"I do not know. Eugene talked little about Claude."

"All right," I said. "You said Danielle was under a bad influence already. You mean Charlie Burgos?"

"You know about that young animal? What does she see in that one? What will he ever be? So arrogant, and so empty!"

"You and Eugene opposed her seeing Charlie Burgos?"

She threw up her hands. "We hated him, but what can a parent do? To forbid her would be a red flag, yes? We said what we thought, but we did not stop her. She will have to learn."

"Could Charlie Burgos have tried to rob the shop?"

"I would believe it, but I think not. He would have known Eugene was there. He would have picked a better time, I think."

"How would Charlie have known Eugene was at the shop?"

"Danielle knew Eugene was staying late."

I nodded. I didn't think Charlie Burgos would have tried.

"What do you know about Jimmy Sung?"

"A sad, lonely man who drinks. But Eugene said he worked very hard, very well."

"Did Eugene play chess with Jimmy Sung?"

"Often. It pleased Eugene very much that Jimmy could play chess. He said Jimmy was good, had learned in some hospital."

"Did he mention playing with Jimmy that night?"

"No. He said nothing about Jimmy."

I shook my head now. "I don't really like the robbery idea, Mrs. Marais, but what else is there? The police have to have at least a hint of some other possible motive."

"Is the fact that Eugene was at the shop that night to meet some-one enough hint, Mr. Fortune?"

"Meet? Who?"

"He did not say who, only that he would be home late because he had to meet someone. He called about six to tell me, and called me again at eleven to say the person had not come. He would wait another hour. That was the last time we spoke."

She sat silent, hearing her husband's last call again.

"Claude?" I said.

"Perhaps. He had seen Claude, expected Claude to return. But I had the impression it was someone else he waited for."

"I met a man at the shop," I said, and described the tall, military type I had bumped into at the shop. "His name could be Paul Manet. Eugene mentioned that name."

"Manet? There was a Paul Manet years ago in Paris, a hero in the Resistance. Eugene knew the family. I did not. If he is in New York, Eugene did not mention it."

"Was Eugene in the Resistance?"

"No, nor did he collaborate. We were small people, we went on living as best we could, as did most."

"How about a Gerd Exner?" I described the scarred German "associate" of Claude Marais.

"I do not know him."

I thought it out. "One more thing. Did Danielle know you were calling me last night, planned to hire me?"

"Yes. She did not approve."

It explained the attack on me in the alley. Charlie Burgos didn't approve of Viviane Marais hiring me, either. Charlie wanted me safely out of action in some hospital.

"Death did not frighten Eugene," Viviane Marais said after a moment. "He said he desired to live long only for me, for us. I do not hate that he is dead, it must happen to all, but I do not believe this robbery. I do not want him to be dead for nothing. Some reason, Mr. Fortune, real or imagined. Not the mindless fiat of a mindless world."

I heard the echo of Marty. Chance was not enough. There must be shape, reason, some conscious direction to life.

"I want you to find that reason," Viviane Marais said. "I have here a hundred dollars. You will bill me for more."

She was a middle-class French housewife, and no one is more practical. I took the money, asked the address of the Balzac Union, and left.

I had a job, and I was beginning to want to know more about the death of Eugene Marais myself. The chaser of theories and puzzles. Maybe Marty was right about me.

6

The Balzac Union was in a brownstone on East Seventeenth Street. A small, quiet lobby with a bust of Napoleon and a portrait of De Gaulle. An old man in some uniform with medals stood behind the desk. There was a bar to the right, a large reading room ahead where affluent-looking men read, played cards, or talked. The events board listed a lot of lectures and discussions.

The director, a tall older man named M. De Lange, met me in his second floor office. His rimless glasses reflected the midday sun through his window, but the office was cool—air-conditioned and pleasant.

"A nice club," I said, as I sat down facing his desk.

"Thank you, Mr. Fortune." His slight accent was English rather than French. "A social club, no politics. The culture of France, and we keep the older people in touch, try to help new arrivals if we can. Kinship and company, shall we say."

"Everyone likes a home," I said.

"If you like," M. De Lange said, his eyes smaller behind the rimless glasses. "But what is it I can do for you?"

"Tell me what you know about Eugene Marais."

He swiveled. "You are a policeman?"

"Private. Mrs. Marais hired me."

"I see." His face became grave. "Very sad. Eugene Marais was not our most active member, although he came often. Not a gregarious man, rather aloof, a watcher of others."

"He wasn't liked much?"

M. De Lange considered. "He was withdrawn, cynical toward our love of things French, a critic of history." The director smiled. "That is not unusual, we French are not a compliant, docile people. Still, many wondered why Eugene joined us."

"Why did he?"

"I suspect to provide an opposition, to prick our bubbles. Eugene admired Balzac, lost no opportunity to remind us that our hero had been a cynic and critic himself. A gadfly, in a way. Most of us associate outside the club, Eugene never did. I don't think he ever invited one of us to his home, for example."

"Any idea why?"

The director removed his rimless glasses, polished them. "He was a psychological hermit, I think. Some past trauma."

"The war? The Occupation? That far back, maybe?"

"Perhaps, but he wasn't a man who talked about himself. So little, one had the feeling he had never done anything at all."

There it was again. As if Eugene Marais somehow made everyone know he had been a man who had done nothing. As if that was important in his mind.

"Is there a Paul Manet in your club, M. De Lange?"

The director almost beamed now. "Indeed. A new member, but not new to us by reputation. How do you know Paul Manet?"

"Eugene Marais mentioned him."

"So? I am surprised. Then, it was the brother who brought Manet to us from San Francisco. They knew each other there."

"Who is Manet that you knew him by reputation?"

"A hero of the Occupation, one who saved many people from the Germans. His name is well known to Frenchmen of that time, as most of us here are."

"What does he do now?"

"A representative of French businesses abroad. A journalist, too, I believe. An imposing man, and a welcome addition here."

"You said he knows Claude Marais. Is Claude a member?"

"No." The director's face clamped shut. He put his glasses back on. "Claude Marais served France well, a hero also, but he is a bitter man turned against all he once fought for. We asked him to join us, of course, but he sneered at us, cursed France to our faces. A misanthrope, unpleasant. Perhaps he has suffered much, is disillusioned, but other men have suffered in defeat and not turned against their country."

"Were Claude and Eugene close? Eugene agreed with Claude?"

"I am not sure. Eugene apologized for Claude, the only time I ever saw Eugene upset, and yet . . . ?" De Lange shrugged. "Eugene said something rather cryptic, then. He said, 'It seems there are different roads to the same end.' And that perhaps there was only one end, life a circle that always came to the same point no matter what road. What he meant, who can say?"

"But Claude Marais rejected your club?"

"And we him. There was an incident. With Paul Manet, in fact. Some of us were discussing Indo-China again, Claude was here, so we asked him to comment, of course. He refused, made remarks about stupidity and cowardice. Manet became angry. There were actual blows, I'm afraid."

"Who won the fight?"

"It was brief," De Lange said uncomfortably. "Claude Marais knocked Paul Manet down."

"Manet's a lot bigger than Claude, looks in good shape."

"Paul Manet is older, and a gentleman."

"Maybe that explains it," I agreed dryly. "Why are you surprised that Eugene Marais mentioned Paul Manet?"

"I did not know they had met. Somehow, Paul Manet was never introduced to Eugene here. Of course, Claude Marais and Manet knew each other in San Francisco, so Eugene must have met Manet on the outside."

On the outside, and a long time ago, maybe, and at least once at the pawn shop—with Claude there even after the fight at this club.

Paul Manet had known the Marais brothers better than the Balzac Union members realized. As if someone wanted the association to remain private.

"You know a man named Gerd Exner?" I asked.

"No. We know few Germans. Stupid, perhaps, but true."

"Where do I find Paul Manet?"

"I believe he sublet an apartment from a member, or was loaned it." De Lange checked a box of file cards. "Here it is: Jules Rosenthal's apartment, 120 Fifth Avenue."

I thanked the director, and left. I walked down. As I passed the desk, the old soldier on duty called to me:

"Monsieur Fortune? Telephone. You take it in the booth."

In the booth I picked up the receiver. "Fortune."

Viviane Marais's voice said, "I thought you would go to the club. A Lieutenant Marx has just called me. He has arrested Jimmy Sung for the robbery and my husband's murder."

Jimmy Sung sat in a straight chair under an overhead light in the hot, dark, windowless interrogation room.

It was bright daylight outside, but in the interrogation room it was always night. A timeless room that could be anywhere. Colorless, bare, with nothing to give it identity, nothing to place it in space, nothing human. A room without a sense of name, and after a time no one in it had a name. In it, as victim or bystander, I felt reduced, stripped. That was the way it was planned.

Two detectives and Lieutenant Marx stood around Jimmy Sung, taking turns talking to him. Another man stood in the shadows. I went to him, expecting to find Captain Gazzo—Homicide chief, and, most of the time, my friend. It wasn't Gazzo. It was a big, heavy man with a pale, massive face and small eyes. Captain Olsen, Narcotics downtown.

"A narcotics angle, Captain?" I said.

"Gazzo's on vacation, I'm filling in on Homicide. You're a lucky man, Fortune. You can collect for doing nothing."

"I won't feel bad," I said. "You're sure, Captain?"

"Listen and find out."

Marx and his two squad men were soft-hammering, casual, putting Jimmy Sung at his ease. It wasn't working.

Jimmy sat rigid in the chair, his soft hands on his thighs under work pants. His feet were flat on the floor, in sneakers, and his back was stiff and straight. His black eyes were fixed straight ahead. He seemed taller, even younger, and his alcoholic eyes were bright. His puffy face had a thin smile. Not amused—a tigerish smile, almost contemptuous. Like a soldier captured by the enemy, waiting for torture, sure they would get nothing from him. I had the illusion that if Jimmy Sung opened his mouth, all that would come out was name, rank and serial number.

"You went to rob the shop," Lieutenant Marx said. "For booze money, right? You didn't know Eugene Marais was there. You had to hit him. You started looting the store, decided to tie Marais up. You found he was dead, panicked, and ran."

Jimmy Sung said nothing, didn't move, his shoulders tense like a man about to be beaten. A man who expects to be beaten.

A detective said, "Come on, Jimmy. We don't think you knew what you were doing. Make it easy."

"We know about those years in that state hospital," the second detective said. "You're not responsible."

The stocky Oriental moved his eyes; black eyes with anger in them now. "A lie, that hospital. You hear?" His eyes looked straight ahead again. "I'm home all night."

I heard it in his voice—colorless, flat. He didn't believe what he had said himself. He didn't believe it, he didn't believe that the police would believe it, but it was his statement. A man who would confess nothing.

Lieutenant Marx sighed, held up a small, jade Buddha. "Here it is, Jimmy. On the list of what was taken from the pawn shop. Found in your apartment. You know it, and we know it."

"Not the same Buddha," Jimmy said.

"It's got Marais's pawn mark on it."

"I never saw it. Someone put it in my place."

"It was in your bookcase, your woman saw it the day after Eugene Marais was killed. You told her it was yours."

"Mr. Marais gave it to me."

"It was still on the inventory, Jimmy."

"Mr. Marais forgot to take it off."

I listened to Jimmy Sung change his claim each time Marx disproved the statement before. Simply, blandly coming up with a totally different claim, and all the time sitting there rigid, his eyes glittering with something peculiarly like pride, waiting for the blows to start. He was denying with his words, changing his claims to meet each charge, but his eyes and body were not denying, not even protesting, simply rejecting. As if he didn't really care what he said, or what was believed. Resigned to be found guilty.

I said, "That Buddha is all you found, Lieutenant?"

"Isn't it enough for you?" Captain Olsen said behind me.

"One piece?" I said to Olsen, to all of them in the dark room. "Where's the rest? Why keep one piece? Come on, it looks to me like some crude frame-up. Jimmy's no thief."

"I'd agree, Dan," Lieutenant Marx said, "if we hadn't also found this at Eugene Marais's shop."

He held a half-pint bottle of vodka. Some brand I'd never heard of. Marx held it in a handkerchief.

"It was on the floor in the backroom, half empty. We found the liquor store clerk who sold it to Jimmy at about ten that night. It was the only half pint he sold, it's a brand only his store carries around here—a cheap brand for bums and alkies. The bottle has Jimmy's prints on it. Clear."

I looked at Jimmy Sung. He still sat unmoving, that thin smile on his face, his bright eyes alert.

"Jimmy's woman says he left his place about nine-fifty. So did she. No one knows when he got home."

In a silence, everyone looked at Jimmy Sung. For a time, he didn't change. Then he licked his lips, lost the thin smile.

"Okay, we played chess. I got there maybe ten o'clock, left maybe eleven o'clock. Mr. Marais was alive. I swear."

A long breath seemed to go through the dark interrogation room. Jimmy had confessed, the denial didn't count. Jimmy had been there, he had had a piece of the stolen property.

"Book him, Marx," Captain Olsen said, and walked out to tend to more important business than Jimmy Sung.

After the two detectives took Jimmy Sung out, small and silent between them, Marx and I sat alone in the interrogation room. I lit a cigarette.

"The rest of the stuff?" I said.

"In the river. In some sewer. We'll look, maybe Jimmy'll tell us now, but it doesn't matter. He's a drunk, Dan, and maybe half crazy, too. When a drunk needs booze money he gets desperate and stupid. We found out that he was in a mental hospital out in California for six years about twenty years ago. It fits, Dan."

It fitted. I went out to call Viviane Marais to tell her the reason her husband had died. She wouldn't like it. Chance, a stupid act of a half-crazy alcoholic. Marty wouldn't like it, either. It would depress her more. Damn!

7

Most men are guilty of the weak hope that if something isn't talked about it will, somehow, go away. I'm no exception, so I didn't tell Marty about Jimmy Sung and how Eugene Marais had died. She heard anyway.

Two days after Jimmy had been booked, the oven-night of the city outside, we were in my bed talking about our vacation plans. I was talking. Marty had been silent for some time. Then she sat up, leaned down over me, and kissed me. She held my shoulders hard—too hard, and a moment too long. It was a kiss that had a lot of years in it, and a decision.

She got out of bed, began to dress. It wasn't quite midnight, not even time to sleep. I lit a cigarette.

"I have to go away, Dan, alone," Marty said. "I have to."

"I have the money, Marty," I said.

"One job. No plan, no growth. You live in space, Dan, not in time. Now is always. Maybe you're right, I don't know."

"When will you know?"

"Probably too late. I'll call you when I get back."

So she went. She would think, but in the end . . . ? A woman doesn't go off alone to think about her relationship to a man unless she has some alternative to think about too.

What Viviane Marais was thinking about I wasn't sure, either. I called her on the phone to tell her about Jimmy Sung the afternoon he was booked. She was silent on the other end for a time.

"Then there is nothing for you to do," she said at last. "Unless you have some doubt, Mr. Fortune?"

Did I have a doubt? Yes and no. Jimmy Sung fitted, and yet there was still the bulk of the stolen goods, Jimmy's weak lying I couldn't understand, and the clumsiness of it all. But all of that could be answered by the confused thinking of an unbalanced drunk, and the police would try to answer it all. They had no axe to grind over Jimmy Sung.

"I don't think I can do much, Mrs. Marais," I said. "So I worked one day. You want fifty dollars back?"

"No, I think not," Viviane Marais said. "So, Jimmy it was? An accident after all? Chance? It would have pleased Eugene."

"But not you?"

"No, but I cannot order the world." She was silent again on the other end of the line. "Keep the money, Mr. Fortune, and if there is some news, call me again."

Everyone was being generous with money. That makes me uneasy. After Marty had gone, I checked to see if Jimmy Sung needed a decent lawyer, or if anything new had happened. Nothing had, and Jimmy had a good lawyer—private, not court appointed. More money from somewhere.

The next few days I spent tracking down a skipped husband for a woman who owned four tenements. The husband had managed the properties, a paid hand. He had vanished without taking any of the cash. That puzzled the woman. The trail ended at Kennedy Airport—tickets for two to Montreal. The second ticket had been used by a dumpy brunette who had hung on the rabbit-husband's arm. The woman-landlord called me off, and even paid me. That gave me over six hundred dollars, rich for me. The money didn't seem very important, somehow.

I was sitting on a bench in Washington Square Park a week after Jimmy's arrest, watching a gang of overage and hairy kids making music in the circle, when the man sat down beside me. Anyone can sit on a bench, for any reason, but this man I watched. Maybe because he was another Oriental. He watched the singers.

"You know Jimmy Sung didn't rob that shop, or kill Mr. Marais," he said.

He was small, slender, in a light brown tropical suit and a hat. Japanese, I decided, but American-Japanese. His English was pure, unaccented American; his voice quiet, even humble. A meditative manner, and no hair came from under his hat as if his head was shaved.

"Why do I know that?" I said.

"Because Jimmy Sung would not steal. Our people do not steal, and Jimmy had no need, anyway. He is hardworking, an industrious man, and has enough money for his needs—all needs."

"Our people?" I said. "Just who are you, Mr.—?"

"Noyoda," the small man said. "I am a Buddhist priest, Mr. Fortune. We have our temple in Chinatown. Jimmy is one of our members. Not very religious, but devoted. He comes to us often, is also paid a small wage as custodian. He would not steal, and if he did not steal, why then would he murder Mr. Marais?"

"Jimmy's a Buddhist?"

"You are surprised?"

"I figured Jimmy as an all-American Chinese."

"In most ways he is," Noyoda said. "Perhaps he felt a certain isolation when he joined us five years ago, I can't say for sure. His life has not been easy or even pleasant, which, I imagine, is why he drinks."

Noyoda seemed to watch the hairy singers in the circle. His face showed no disapproval, nor any approval, only a kind of understanding, as if his meditations embraced all things alive.

"Jimmy was brought from China as a boy. He talks little, but from things he has said I think he was almost a slave of the man who brought him to America. It seems there was some trouble in his late teens with this employer's daughter. Some drinking, a fight, and Jimmy was locked in a mental hospital for six years. He was alone, without friends or visitors, the entire six years because no one could communicate with him. Schizophrenic was the diagnosis because Jimmy was silent or seemed to babble in gibberish. You see, at that time, Jimmy spoke only a Manchurian dialect, and no one understood a word of it!

"He would probably still be there, as has happened to others, if a new doctor at the hospital hadn't happened to have worked in North China and recognized a few words Jimmy mumbled at rare times. The doctor found a man who spoke Jimmy's language, and at last Jimmy could tell his story. He recovered his speech rapidly then, and they released him—with a few dollars, one suit, no skills and no friends anywhere. That was when he began to be an alcoholic."

I watched the singers and guitar players in the circle. Some of them were dancing now. Some were grabbing each other, getting together for the night to come, and maybe even longer.

"It's enough to do it," I said. "Alkie or worse."

"Since then," Noyoda said, "he supported himself, taught himself English, took nothing from anyone. A strict, austere, frugal life. Hard-working and never in trouble, not even drunk. Such a man does not steal, and certainly never for pennies. He is not stupid, Mr. Fortune. If he had robbed that shop he would have taken more and not been so clumsy."

Two policemen had appeared under the arch of the square, and in the circle the ragged youth-sing was breaking up.

"Could he have faked a clumsy robbery to cover murder?"

"What possible reason could Jimmy have? Mr. Marais was his friend and employer. Jimmy liked the job at the shop."

"What motives does anyone have?" I said morosely.

"I thought that perhaps you could find that out."

Everyone wanted to hire me. Maybe I could make a career out of Eugene Marais's death. One small pawn shop owner.

Noyoda said, "The members of our temple have contributed what they can. We wish to help Jimmy. We planned to hire a lawyer for him, but he has one, and we thought that we could use the money to hire you to prove his innocence."

"Jimmy paid for his own lawyer? How?"

"No, someone else hired the lawyer. I heard it was Claude Marais, the brother. Perhaps he thinks Jimmy innocent too."

That made me sit up. "All right, but one thing still bothers me—the way Jimmy kept on lying even when Lieutenant Marx had him cold. The way he lied about being there at all that night."

"Given his life, Mr. Fortune, it is understandable that he is somewhat paranoid, isn't it? Wary and silent."

"Maybe it is," I said. "You can pay me fifty dollars now."

Money is money, and, with Marty gone, what else did I have to do?

I rode the Hotel Stratford elevator straight up to the fourth floor and room 427. Li Marais opened the door.

"Mr. Fortune?"

She wore a western mini-skirt and blouse now, and I saw again how wrong I had been about her fragility. Her legs were far from fragile.

"Can I talk to your husband?"

"Come in, please."

The room was a small living room with the usual anonymous furniture of a second-rank but respectable hotel. There was a bedroom and a tiny kitchenette. A suite for more permanent residence. A lot of people in New York lived in residential hotels like the Stratford.

"Claude is not here, but perhaps I can help," she said.

She sat down, crossed her legs. Her thighs were smooth and full. I sat on a couch.

"Why did Claude hire a lawyer for Jimmy Sung? Doesn't he think Jimmy killed Eugene after all?"

"Claude did not hire the lawyer, I did," she said, her dark eyes bright and on my face. "I sold some jewels, Claude gave me some money. It was something I felt I must do."

"Why?"

"Since Claude and I came to New York, Jimmy has been nice to me, always helping. Small things—favors, errands, services, company

46

when I've been alone. Perhaps because I speak his old language, but the reason does not matter."

"I thought you were Thai?"

"A Thai orphan adopted by a Chinese family in Vietnam. Life is a flux these last long years in Southeast Asia, death and change are what we know. The people who took me in were from North China. Saigon is a crossroad. I speak most Oriental languages now, as well as French and my little English."

"You speak a lot of English."

She smiled. It was her first smile, soft and warm. "Thank you, but I do not speak as well as even poor Jimmy. He helped my English, too. He seemed to like to talk to me, a memory of his forgotten past, perhaps."

"Do you think he robbed the shop, killed Eugene?"

"My help does not depend on what he did or did not do. He helped me in a strange city. A lonely man who understands the loneliness in others."

"Are you lonely, Mrs. Marais?"

Her expression didn't change, she had no outward mannerisms, but I sensed a faint change in her whole body. Something in her bright eyes that considered me, probed behind my face. She smoothed her skirt—the universal gesture of a woman aware of herself, of her body. Touched herself.

"My husband was a soldier, a patriot, a man of loyalty and courage and devotion," she said slowly. "All of this he put into the cause of France, and France lost. That hurt him, but it was not the worst. He came to believe that France had deserved to lose, that the world of France and honor was dead, and now he has no world he can understand. He cannot believe in France, or America, or China, or any country or cause. No pride, no destiny, no purpose."

"Is he a man who needs a purpose?"

"Most men are. Even you, I think, if only to do your work well. Claude has no work to do well. He works to keep us alive, no more. Sometimes I am sure he does not even know where he is—here or

Saigon; Paris or the jungle." Her eyes seemed to look into me from a hollow inside herself. "He is alone, Dan, can feel nothing. Not war or peace, hate or love."

Her face told me that she knew she had called me Dan. My mouth was dry. Maybe because of Marty, but I wanted this woman, and in her own way she was saying that her loneliness needed help. What kind of help maybe she wasn't sure herself.

I said, "How long have you been married, Li?"

"Eighteen years." She watched me. "I was twelve when I married Claude. A few months before Dienbienphu. It is not uncommon in Vietnam, as your own soldiers have found. A child is a good wife for a soldier. Better than the brothels, or older women who want only his money and disappear when he goes to fight. A child will not leave him. Children die so easily in Asia, have no food, no medicine, no doctors, no homes. A child must work early, is easily lost in war. Vietnamese love children, and to be married is to be safe, fed, even happy. It is better for a child to be a wife than an ox."

"Afterward? When you weren't twelve anymore? Now?"

"I was Madame Marais, I was content. We lived many places, and Claude fought and worked for France. Now he is wasted as the land is wasted, burned out like the villages of Vietnam."

Her small hands lay flat on her thighs, squeezed.

"Why did you hire me to stop Gerd Exner that night?"

"I hoped you would make him go away, leave the country. He hates to be noticed, watched. I hoped you would scare him."

"I scared him, but he stayed around. Why? Who is Exner? Is there something he wants from Claude?"

"He is an ex-Legionnaire. Claude worked with him in Vietnam and Africa—trading, arms smuggling, black market. I do not know why he stays. I only wanted to help Claude. Eugene once said that Claude must wipe the past away, forget and start over. I had hoped to make Exner go away, make Claude forget."

What she had hoped was to have her man back. If it wasn't too late.

"Could Eugene have gotten in Exner's way somehow? Maybe gotten in Claude's way?"

I saw that the thought had occurred to her too. A shadow of possible motives she didn't want to think about. I saw more on her face— an awareness of me. But she said nothing, only sat like some earth-mother who could only wait, had always waited, silent and still, for what would be done to her.

After a time I got up and left.

8

In her black dress, Viviane Marais stood at the door of the old frame house in Sheepshead Bay with a glass of wine in her hand.

"So?" the widow said. "Come in, Mr. Fortune."

She took me into the spotless living room where everything shined as if she'd spent each day since Eugene Marais had died cleaning. She offered me a glass of the wine—La Tache, a fine, heavy Burgundy. I didn't say no. I sat, sipped.

"You're not surprised to see me?" I said.

"No."

"You don't believe Jimmy Sung killed Eugene?"

"One can tell a man who will steal. Jimmy Sung would not. Too much pride. If he did not steal, what reason is there?"

"Why didn't you say that when I told you Jimmy was accused?"

She drank her glass empty, poured a fresh glass. "Eugene always said that only a man's will counted—to do something for yourself, not for others or for gain. If I had told you to go on it would have been a job, for money. I wanted to see if you would come to me from your own doubts."

"You know your sister-in-law hired a lawyer for Jimmy?"

"Li is a strong woman, she has her beliefs."

"And her troubles?"

"Yes, and her troubles."

"With Claude her main trouble?"

She tasted her wine as if it were thick enough to chew, savored it. "Eugene said once that Claude is like a man who has done some awful crime and now waits for his punishment—paralyzed. He treats

50

Li like a sister, a daughter. What woman can live like that? Married eighteen years and not yet thirty-one?"

"She needs a husband again," I said.

"So?" Viviane Marais said. "She has let you see that?"

"Doesn't she usually let anyone see that?"

"No," the widow said, watched me. "Treat her well, Mr. Fortune. She is a warm woman, loyal. A man who finds her with him will be lucky."

I thought so too, and Marty was off somewhere making her decision, but I changed the subject for now.

"Some crime Claude had on his mind, Eugene said," I said. "Could Eugene have meant some real crime? In Claude's past?"

"I don't know," Viviane Marais said. "At the time I thought Eugene meant it only as a metaphor, but now—?"

"Could Claude be involved in something illegal? Some deal Eugene might have discovered, maybe tried to stop?"

"What Claude might be doing I can't know," the widow said. "But Eugene would not try to stop anything. He had seen too much of the horror caused by righteous men who think that they must stop other men for some abstract truth, for some principle."

"What if he found that Claude was using *him* in some way?" I said. "Had involved him in some scheme?"

"Eugene would not have permitted that, but he would not have done anything against Claude, either."

"Maybe Claude, or Gerd Exner, didn't know that," I said.

She thought, sipped her good wine, shrugged. There were too many "ifs," but the possibility hung in the room.

"This Paul Manet," I said. "You said Eugene had known him in the past in Paris?"

"Eugene knew the Manet family. I do not know if he knew Paul or not, or how well. Paul Manet was active in the Resistance, Eugene was not."

"What is Vel d'Hiv?" I said. "Why would Paul Manet not want to talk about it? Why would it make him jumpy?"

"How do you know Paul Manet did not want to talk about it?"

"Claude said that to Eugene the day he was killed."

She finished her wine again, did not refill her glass this time. She watched the far wall. "On the night of July 16, 1942, the Gestapo and the Paris police rounded up twelve thousand or so Jews, imprisoned them like sheep in the sports stadium—the Vélodrome d'Hiver; to us: Vel d'Hiv. Non-French Jews, mostly German and Polish refugees. They were there a week, a hell, before they were sent to the worst hell of Auschwitz. It is not an episode most Frenchmen over forty-five want to talk about." She reached for the wine bottle. "Four thousand of those Jews were children."

She poured her glass of wine. Not new, no, one of thousands of such episodes in those barbarian years of the Third Reich, and that was why the silence of the neat living room in Sheepshead Bay was so brutal—I could imagine the scene, visualize it from a million other stories, reports, pictures. I could see and hear the bewildered suffering of those refugee children.

"Were Paul Manet and Eugene involved somehow?" I said.

"Eugene was not himself. We are half-Jewish, Eugene was at least, but French Jews were not affected. Some . . . friends were." she drank. "Paul Manet risked his own life to warn many of the refugees, and rescued some. He is not a Jew, and it was a great risk in those days."

"Eugene did nothing? Took no part?"

"He did nothing," the widow said.

"Paul Manet would have no hatred against him, blame him for anything? Eugene had nothing against Manet?"

"I cannot think what. Few ordinary Frenchmen were part of it that night. Eugene did nothing bad, and Paul Manet was a hero. What could there be?"

She had no reason to be lying. Eugene Marais was dead, if he had done anything on that long-ago night to cause his murder now, she would have no reason to hide it and protect his killer. Or would she? Some guilty secret so bad . . . ? No, Eugene Marais had not been a man to evade his own guilt.

"Does Danielle think Jimmy Sung guilty?" I said.

"How can I say what Danielle thinks?" Viviane Marais said.

"Has she seemed to doubt Jimmy's guilt at all?"

"No, she has not. She has said nothing. Why?"

"I'm pretty sure Charlie Burgos tried to have me beaten up to get me off the case, and he's got Danielle up-tight about something. If he didn't rob the shop, kill Eugene, and you didn't try to stop Danielle seeing him, what interest does he have in it all? Could he have been the one Eugene was meeting that night?"

"I have no idea, Mr. Fortune."

I rubbed at my stump, it was aching. "All right, you're sure Jimmy Sung isn't a thief, not the type. But what facts do we have to support that? Some concrete proof it wasn't Jimmy?"

"Jimmy cares nothing about money, really. Eugene paid him well, too much, and often Jimmy would leave on payday without his money. As long as he had money in his pocket for his bottle that night. Also, he worked in the shop, *hein?* He knew where any money was, how much there was in the shop. Would he not have gone straight to the money first? He had, too, the combination of the safe. Would he not have opened the safe at once?"

"Unless he knew Eugene was dead as soon as he hit him, and panicked at once," I said, and answered my own question before she could. "No, then he would have just run, no point to taking anything at all. And the killer didn't know Eugene was dead, or he wouldn't have tied him to that chair."

"No, Jimmy never needed money that much, Mr. Fortune," Viviane Marais said.

"Everyone needs money that much, Mrs. Marais," I said.

9

The six-story old-law tenement off Ninth Avenue wasn't a lot different from my building. No shabbier than most buildings in Chelsea, and in some ways a lot cleaner—the steps swept and washed, the outer door painted, even a few geraniums in sidewalk boxes now wilted in the heat.

Jimmy Sung lived on the fourth floor, the stairs swept and dusted. I knocked, expecting no answer. But I got one. A woman opened Jimmy Sung's door. A plain woman, almost ugly, and bone thin. A cheap print dress hung on her bones like a sack, and she wore old sneakers for shoes, but her skin was bright and clear for her age—maybe fifty—and there was a snap to her brown eyes that said she wasn't a woman who gave up on life easily. A vigor in her, tenacious, despite the fact that she had been crying.

"Yeh?" A wary voice, protective. She dabbed her eyes.

"This is Jimmy Sung's apartment?" I said.

She nodded. "He's in jail. No key. Go—"

"I know where he is," I said. "My name's Dan Fortune, a private detective working on the Marais murder."

"What's to work on?" she said, but she left the door open as she walked back into the apartment.

I followed into a windowless living room smaller than my own—and a lot neater. An almost bare room, clean and scrubbed, like the cell of some ascetic monk. A daybed couch without cushions, the wall for a back rest; two high-backed wooden armchairs of the kind they sell for rustic lawn furniture; one lamp from some junkyard; a wooden table and three kitchen chairs. The woman didn't sit, she leaned against a wall, lit a cigarette, one eye half closed against the smoke that drifted up.

"Nobodies like Jimmy are always guilty," she said, her open eye fixed on my face. "Isn't it over? Sure it is."

"Maybe,' I said. "Some of us aren't so sure."

"Forget the forgotten," she said. "Mentally homeless, the only world left is inside. They turn the key, the end."

"You're his woman?"

"Marie Schmidt. Drunky Marie. I'm not even my own woman." She took the cigarette from her lips, picked tobacco. "Yeh, I'm his woman. I told them about that Buddha. My big mouth. You really think he's got a chance?"

"If he didn't do it. I'll need help."

"Help? What, witnesses to say he was somewhere else? All the people who remember a drunk Chinese on the street? His business partners, wife, children, friends, alumni brothers? How about a magician?"

"Did anyone see him that night?"

She laughed. "Nobody ever sees him. Just a Chink. Six years in a damned insane asylum because he couldn't speak—"

"I know about that," I said.

"Okay, you know. It was never much different for Jimmy outside that booby hatch. Who knows him? Who talks to him? The neighborhood Chink. Most people act like he's got no real right to speak English or be alive here. No big discrimination, you know, no real bigotry. Just that he doesn't really exist, they don't even see him. All except Mr. Marais, he was nice, a friend. So it got to be him they say Jimmy killed!"

She stopped, sighed, found an ashtray for her cigarette. "That Buddha, you know? He put it back there in the bedroom the day after Mr. Marais was killed—to honor Mr. Marais, he said. He said Mr. Marais gave it to him, and he put it in the bookcase and lighted incense in front of it. He sat down on the floor looking at it for an hour without saying anything."

She was silent as if seeing Jimmy Sung silent in front of the small Buddha. "I never saw it before, and I told the cops. I don't know how long Jimmy had it, but the cops say it proves he just got it from the shop the night of the murder. If he got it that way, you'd think he'd hide it, not bring it out."

"You would," I said, "if he's sane. Is he sane?"

"Who is?" she said. "He's not crazy, Fortune. Not perfect, but not crazy more than anyone. He gets moody, who doesn't? Sometimes when he's drunk he gets mad and says I got the wrong eyes, I'm not a Chink. Hell, I get mad and call him a Chink. That doesn't make me crazy or a murderer."

"You live here, Marie?"

"Here? Hell no!" She looked for another cigarette, lit one. "Like I said, who's perfect? He's a Chink, I couldn't live with him, you know? Maybe I'm ashamed, but he's all I've got, and I want him back."

As she'd said, no one is perfect, and no one can escape their past, their culture, completely. She'd gone a long way, she had her Chinese man, but the past dies hard and slow.

"I'll do my best," I said. "You said he left here at nine-fifty that night. Did he say where he was going?"

"No, he never says. That's his hang-up—tell no woman. A man does what he feels like, okay?"

"Did anyone see him anywhere after eleven o'clock that night? He says he left the pawn shop at eleven o'clock, Marais was alive."

"If anyone saw him, no one's told me."

"You weren't here after ten o'clock anyway?"

"No, not until next morning. He was asleep when I came."

It was no help at all. "Can I look over the apartment?"

"Why not?" Marie Schmidt said.

There were three other railroad rooms—a bedroom with windows at the front as clean and bare as the living room: a double bed with sheets but no cover, and no blanket in a New York summer; two wooden chairs; a stained bureau; and a large bookcase with books in English and Chinese. On the third shelf of the bookcase there was an open niche that was empty except for a small, bronze saucer with incense ash in it—where the Buddha that sent Jimmy to jail had been.

A windowless middle room set up with a mattress on the floor, two low, Oriental chairs, and a television set.

A rear room bright with the late afternoon sun through backyard windows. A totally empty room. Some shelves, hooks on the walls, and nothing else.

"He usually keeps this room locked," Marie Schmidt said behind me. "Burglars. The fire escape's out there, and Jimmy was afraid of burglars. They might steal his treasures."

She looked behind her at the bare, cheap furniture. She shook her head as if she would never understand people or life. She wasn't alone in that feeling.

"Even here, four rooms don't cost peanuts," I said. "Did Jimmy make enough money for this and his booze?"

"Not money," Marie Schmidt said. "Work. He helps the super, gets free rent. That's why this building is clean, painted. He doesn't pay for much except booze, he works for it. He likes work. See what it's gotten him?"

10

I called Lieutenant Marx before I went down to the prison, and when I got there they were expecting me. Marx had said I could see Jimmy Sung—with Jimmy's lawyer.

The lawyer was a big, energetic-looking man with a heavy briefcase and eyes sunk deep in the heavy black sockets of a man who rarely got enough sleep. His name was Kandinsky. He wanted to know what I had. I told him. It wasn't much, but Kandinsky hadn't expected much.

"The wife too?" the lawyer said. "The sister-in-law hires me, the wife hires you. Good, I can use that."

"His priest hired me too, swears by Jimmy," I said.

"A Buddhist kook won't carry much weight with a jury sure to be half-Catholic, half-Jewish," Kandinsky said seriously, "but the wife thinking he didn't do it is good. I can deal with that. With no real motive, a shaky case on the robbery, that bad deal out in the California nut house, and the victim's wife and sister-in-law on our side, the D.A.'ll have to deal. I can get delays and rulings forever. He'll settle for a minimum charge, and a guilty plea. Clear the calendar. Five years tops."

"How about if I prove him innocent?"

"Well, that's the hard way, but go ahead and try," Kandinsky said. "That all you have?"

"That's all."

The lawyer nodded, and when Jimmy was brought into the visitors room, gave the stocky Chinese a reassuring smile.

"It's good, Jimmy. I'm sure I can deal for you. Behave yourself, get some sleep. I've got four more clients to see today, okay?"

The lawyer's smile seemed to still be in the room after he had gone. I watched Jimmy. The stocky man's broad, pale-brown face revealed nothing, not even the alcoholic's torture inside without his liquor. His dark eyes blinked at the door where Kandinsky had left. His work-gnarled fingers ran through his thinning gray hair—the only sign of any nerves.

"He's a good lawyer?" Jimmy said.

"I'd say so," I said. "He must be costing Li Marais a lot."

Jimmy nodded, didn't smile. "She's a good woman, sure. I know. We understand."

"Kandinsky'll deal for you, Jimmy. I'd like to get the truth. Tell me the whole story, okay?"

"Truth?" Jimmy Sung's dark eyes were immobile. "What truth you mean, Mr. Fortune? I told the cops all I know."

"And a lot of lies," I said. "You were there that night?"

"Okay, yeh. I got there maybe ten o'clock. For chess. We played some. I left around eleven o'clock. Mr. Marais was okay."

"The game was over? With the chess set still up?"

Jimmy licked at his lips. "Mr. Marais got a call. Some guy coming to see him. No time to finish the game. I left."

"What man was coming to see him?"

"I don't know."

"His brother? Claude Marais?"

"He was there before I got there."

"He was supposed to come back."

"No one told me about it. Mr. Marais he expected someone, he didn't tell me who. The call was the guy he expected."

The stocky Chinese spoke short and flat, each statement without overtones. No tone of question, no fervor of innocence. Not uninterested, but saying that he was telling all he could, and that was all. His normal manner, flat and brief, but now his left hand had begun to twitch, clench.

"Did you see the man Eugene Marais expected, Jimmy?"

"I was gone."

"Were you drunk, Jimmy?"

"Maybe some."

"By ten o'clock? When do you usually start drinking? Maybe five-thirty? Six o'clock? Four and a half hours?"

"My woman was with me, Marie. She holds me down. I took it slow. The chess game, you know? That's how come I took a bottle with me to the shop. I was drunk some, not bad."

The middle-aged Chinese's left hand went on with its nervous jumping. He didn't hold it, or try to stop it. He didn't seem to notice it. I had the feeling that no matter where or when I talked to Jimmy Sung he would be the same—locked deep inside some thick shell where only he lived. Even the drab prison clothes looked much the same as his day-to-day clothes.

"Where did you go after eleven or so, Jimmy?"

"Some bars. I told the cops. They don't believe me. No one says they saw me."

"Did anyone see you who knew you?"

"No one knows me much. I drink in a booth. A lot of bars."

"No regular tavern?"

"No. Except where I work sweeping. I don't go to those."

"Tell me the bars," I said.

"Fugazy's Tavern, Packy's Pub, the Tugboat. The cops been there already."

"You never know when you'll get lucky," I said. "You saw no one else at the pawn shop that night?"

"The girl come in, Danielle. With her kid, that Charlie Burgos. Mr. Marais tossed them out before I left."

"What did they want?"

"I don't know. They was always bugging Mr. Marais. No good punk kids. No respect. Too damned weak, Mr. Marais."

I heard the change in his voice before it showed on his broad face. A crack in the flat monotone, a catch like some liquid in his throat, and then the wet dark eyes. His jumping left hand brushed at his eyes. Whatever it was, it was no act. An edge of tears.

"This city, I got no friends. No one. I got no name, but he was my friend, Mr. Marais. He gave me work, paid me good. I work good for him, now he got to die. He ain't like most of them. French, too, but he treats me good. That Buddha he give me, free, so when he's dead I pray to it, burn incense. For him. He'll be okay. He was my friend."

What did it mean? I've seen killers cry for their victims before. Too many times, the murderous moment gone. I've even seen them forget who did the killing. Yet, Eugene Marais had been Jimmy Sung's friend, and where was a motive for murder?

"You've got friends, Jimmy. Li Marais. Claude. The widow. Me, I hope. Marie Schmidt. She's a strong woman, I think."

"A drunk. Like me," Jimmy Sung said, the moment of tears past. "She got no one else but me. A Chink sweeps floors."

"She's waiting for you," I said.

"Yeh, Marie's okay."

"She wasn't there when you got home that night? What time?"

"Who knows. By then I'm drunk. I sleep late."

"You're sure no one saw you after eleven o'clock?"

Jimmy Sung only shrugged. Who would remember him?

11

The police had combed the three bars before me, as Jimmy Sung had said. At Fugazy's they had been crowded that night, no one remembered seeing Jimmy Sung, or any Chinaman—only in Fugazy's, where the barmen did know Jimmy, they didn't think of Jimmy as a Chinaman. You can lose all ways. I know. When I want my missing arm noticed, no one seems to have thought about it.

At Packy's Pub they had been slow enough the murder night, and everyone who'd been there was *sure* Jimmy hadn't been in. Of course, they all said they didn't know Jimmy Sung hardly.

A "Chink" had maybe been in the Tugboat Grill, but in the Tugboat all Chinks looked alike, okay?

Maybe someone had seen Jimmy Sung that night in one of the bars, but it could take years to dig one witness out of the nameless regulars and faceless transients who fill Chelsea bars. Even then, it would prove only that part of Jimmy Sung's story was true. Eugene Marais could have been dead by eleven that night. What I needed was someone to say Eugene had been alive at eleven o'clock. Someone other than Jimmy Sung.

There was no more police seal on the pawn shop door. With Jimmy Sung in jail, the police had all they wanted from the shop—at least, officially. As I took out my ring of keys to open the shop door, a black car glided to a stop at the curb.

"Something on your mind, Fortune?" a voice said from the back seat of the car.

Captain Olsen, the Narcotics chief filling in at Homicide for Gazzo. He was slouched in the back seat, a big shadow with a pale, massive face half hidden. His small eyes caught random light from the busy avenue. His driver looked straight ahead.

"Fishing, Captain. Everybody seems to want to pay me, but I've got my doubts anyway. That Buddha is just too dumb."

"It was dumb," Olsen agreed. "We haven't found any of the rest of the loot. You can skip the alleys around here, we've vacuumed them all."

"Jimmy could have dumped the loot ten miles away, kept the Buddha by accident," I said.

"Sure he could have," Captain Olsen said. But I heard it; Olsen had doubts too. If you don't run head-on into their prejudices, the cops can do very good work.

"You've checked everywhere he went the day after?"

"Ten times."

"You know, Captain," I said, "it's an awful funny bag of loot for a burglary. Junk, and no real pattern to it."

"It's a funny bag," Olsen said. "Tell us what you find."

The bulky Captain tapped his window. The driver started the car, eased away heading downtown. Olsen had other work, but now I knew this case was bothering him. They were still at work, arrest or no arrest. It was hopeful. If I found anything at all, the police would at least listen.

Two hours later I sat down at Eugene Marais's silent desk and lit a cigarette. The desk was exactly as it had been the morning we found the pawn shop owner dead. So was the whole shop. Viviane Marais had not been in, it was too soon.

It hadn't helped me. In the two hours I had found nothing at all to back Jimmy Sung's story, or to show that anyone else had been in the shop. A pawn shop is a hard place to find clues. Too much junk. Anything could be meaningful or meaningless.

The back door locked with a bolt. It had been locked that morning, it was still locked. The alley cobbles showed nothing. The locked safe and overlooked cash drawer still stared at me. Eugene Marais's papers and account books didn't show he had given a Buddha to Jimmy Sung, but they didn't show he hadn't, either. Nothing had been written down about Paul Manet, or Claude Marais and his wife, or Charlie Burgos, or anyone.

I smoked, and looked around the back room, and looked out into the shop, and read the list of loot again. Not at once, not sudden, the odd fact seeped into my mind. There all along, it wasn't exactly a bolt of lightning. In police work, not much is. Just something that began to chew at my slow mind as I saw a high shelf of suitcases in the back room. A vacant space in the row of suitcases sort of winked at me.

I rechecked the list of loot. Yes, one suitcase was on the list. Last entry. Naturally, all the missing junk had to be carried away in something. Obvious, very normal, of course.

For a burglar who came to rob the pawn shop?

A burglar planning to loot a pawn shop, stopped by an unintended murder, but with robbery in mind before he arrived?

If I planned a robbery, I'd bring my own bag for the loot. Wouldn't anyone? Panic? But no bag or sack had been found in the shop. Only a missing suitcase from stock. So? So maybe it had not been a planned robbery at all.

I stubbed out my cigarette, lit another. Okay, I'd be scientific—make an assumption and see what it gave me. Assume—the killer did *not* come to rob the pawn shop. Why did he rob it, then? To make it look like a robbery-murder. A cover to hide the real motive. Illusion to make us look the wrong way.

Okay, did it help me? Who, why, when? No. Then what?

Well, if it was robbery only for cover, then the killer had no interest in the loot, didn't care a damn about it. In fact, the loot was a danger to the killer. He would dump it fast.

Get rid of the loot before anyone caught him with it—but not so that it could be found easily. That could spoil the robbery illusion. So, get rid of it, make sure it wasn't traceable to him, but make sure no one found it soon or ever.

Over a week now, and no loot found. So it had been well hidden—if I was right. Not in an alley nearby, not just tossed into a street—too easy for a chance pick-up and turn-in. Some garbage can? Garbage men look into suitcases, scavengers work all over the city hoping for a find like a suitcase, and the loot was a suspiciously odd bag. The sewers would be the first place the police would look, a suitcase doesn't fit down a grating, and a man feeding handfuls into a sewer would be a stand-out sight.

A killer in a hurry to fade away. A suitcase of loot. Get rid of it nearby, make sure it couldn't be traced back, and not have it found, hopefully, ever. Where?

A railroad baggage room? Police might check. Terminal or subway coin locker? Removed too soon, opened, reported. Hotel room, unclaimed baggage? They'd open the suitcase to look for identification and some address, and the contents would be very suspicious. Salvation Army? Maybe—but midnight or later?

Where?

12

I dropped the suitcase on Lieutenant Marx's desk at nine-thirty the next morning. I'd had a good night's sleep, and I was feeling good. As good as I could with Marty still gone and silent.

"It's all there," I said, "except two watches that were sold. I checked the list."

Marx opened the bag. "Sold? Two watches?"

"Salvation Army," I said. "It was turned over to a porter at the men's flophouse near Cooper Square around one A.M. the night of the murder. Neat and smart, Marx. The man who handed it to the porter said he'd cleaned out his store, was leaving town early the next day, didn't have time to go to the big main store, but wanted the Salvation Army to have the stuff. The mission people sent it to the big store the next day."

I lit a cigarette. "I was on the doorstep this morning when they opened. They had a record of the donation, it took an hour to round up the stuff on the list. The two watches were sold, but that accounts for all of it except the Buddha. If Jimmy Sung had pulled a smart trick like taking it all to that mission, would he have kept out the Buddha you'd be sure to find and trace to the list of loot? No."

"You can't be sure, Dan. A drunk like Jimmy," Marx said, but I could hear that his heart wasn't really in it now.

"I can be sure," I said. "That porter who took the bag at the mission is a black wino. He was half in the bag, never really saw the man's face to remember, but he's sure of one thing if you want to get him down here."

"What's he sure of?"

"That the generous donator was a 'whitey,' yessir. 'Ofay all the way, sure not one of our yellow brothers!' Couldn't say what the cat looked like, but he was sure a whitey."

"A wino won't stand up as a witness."

"He will with the rest, with Kandinsky breathing hard. Go ask the D.A. Jimmy didn't take that loot, Marx."

Marx looked at the suitcase. "You've got luck, Dan."

"Sometimes it takes a little luck," I said. "Your jails are full of poor slobs, guilty and innocent, who had no luck."

"No system's perfect," Marx said.

"Besides, it wasn't all luck. Science, deduction, right?" I said. "Here's some more deductions. Jimmy Sung isn't the kind of man who'd steal, and now you've got the loot and a man who says Jimmy didn't have it. Jimmy's not a stupid man, he wouldn't have kept that Buddha from the loot, so Eugene Marais had to have given it to him as he says. If Jimmy had robbed that store, he'd have taken the cash, opened the safe. No jury will believe Jimmy Sung robbed the shop now, and what other motive could he have? Eugene Marais was his friend, a benefactor. We've got to believe, now, that Eugene was alive when Jimmy left. You can't hold him, Lieutenant. You had some doubts anyway."

"I guess so," Marx said after a moment. "So the robbery was a cover for murder. We did wonder."

"A panic job, sloppy. If you wondered, maybe you were working on something else? What?"

Marx shook his head. "Nothing sure, not yet. Just a few doubts. Keep working."

I was waiting downtown when Jimmy Sung came out. He blinked in the sun, like one of his own Buddhas in work clothes, but didn't stop walking. I fell in step along the hot, noontime street of the crowded, hurrying city.

"I want to talk to you, Jimmy."

"I need a drink," he said, not even looking at me.

He went straight to the first bar like a homing pigeon. The bartender served him his double vodka. Now his hands shook as he carried the glass to an empty booth in the long room of businessmen. I ordered a beer. In the booth, Jimmy took a long drink. And a second. Then he set the glass down, breathed.

"They let me go, hey?"

"They had to. You never robbed that shop."

"You?"

"I helped, found the loot. They had doubts anyway."

"No, you. Thanks." He drank again.

"Thank the Marais women. They believed you."

"Sure." He finished his vodka.

"Jimmy, I want you to think about that night again. You were the only one to see Eugene Marais after ten o'clock."

"That Charlie Burgos and Danielle was there."

"But left before you. After that, you were the last to see Eugene Marais alive. You're sure you don't remember anything more than you've told me already?"

"Lerame think."

Jimmy stood, walked to the bar. His hands were no longer shaking. He paid for another double vodka, came back to the booth. He drank, shook his head.

"No more than I told you. I left at eleven sharp, ran the bars, got drunk, went home." He drank. "Maybe I saw Danielle and that Burgos out on the avenue around then, I ain't sure."

"Doing what?"

He drank. "Nothing. Just hanging around."

I drank. "Okay, Jimmy. Who killed him? Any ideas? You knew him. Any enemies? Threats? Worried about anything."

"Last week or so, he was kind of moody."

"About what?"

"I don't know, just something on his mind. Thinking about something. I need a drink."

He went to the bar again. This time he had to count out change for his double vodka. He'd need me for a drink soon. When he came back, he was already swaying a little—the quick drunk of the alcoholic. He might pass out in ten minutes, or he might remain half drunk all day.

I said, "Was Eugene worried about Claude? Could Claude be mixed up in something? Maybe Eugene got in the way?"

"He worried about that Claude, all right. Didn't like him around the girl, Danielle; didn't like how he lived, doing nothing. I don't know about anything maybe happening."

"You know anything about a Gerd Exner?"

Jimmy shook his head, drank. He was staring into his glass, his eyes dulling, filming over with the alcohol. I didn't have a lot of time to get something from him. Then, you never knew about an alcoholic. Sometimes they functioned long after they seemed out on their feet.

"How about Paul Manet?" I said.

"Manet?" Jimmy blinked into his glass, the Oriental eyes closing. "Maybe I heard some name like that. I don' know." He shook his head, drank. "I don' know."

I described the tall, aristocratic ex-hero. "He was in the shop around five the murder night."

"Yeh, I remember. He closed the door when he was talking to Mr. Marais in the back room. That Claude come in, left the door open. They was talking about France, the old days, all like that. I didn't pay much notice. Some funny name, too."

"Vel d'Hiv?"

"Maybe. Something like that."

"Were they angry, arguing?"

"I don' know. I left pretty soon. After that Claude come in." Jimmy drank, his head down now, hanging forward, the glass almost missing his mouth. "That Claude! No good, that one. Big hero. Medals for killin' peasants, coolies! Big Frenchie hero kills kids, marries girl-babies got no home. Bad man, no good. Steal women, steal everything!"

"Steal what, Jimmy? What did Claude Marais steal?"

"Everything," Jimmy said, nodded violently, his vodka spilling over. "No good, Mr. Marais says so. No good."

"What did Eugene say? Jimmy?"

He looked up at me, one eye closed, the open eye bright with drunken cunning. "Buy me a drink."

I bought a double vodka, came back. "What did Eugene say?"

"Something," Jimmy said, drank. "That Claude give him something. To hold. Who knows?"

His shoulders were down, his arms limp, a drunk smile on his broad face. I left him there. He was too far gone now. I didn't try to get him home, he wouldn't have gone. He could get home himself. He'd been doing it a long time.

13

At the Hotel Stratford desk, my clerk-friend, George Jenkins, told me that Li and Claude Marais had gone out together. I sat down in a corner of the small lobby to wait. I hadn't eaten any breakfast, in a hurry to get to the Salvation Army warehouse store, and the beer I'd had with Jimmy Sung was sloshing in emptiness. George Jenkins sent a bellman out to get me a sandwich.

I'd finished it, was thinking of maybe another, when Li Marais came into the lobby. She was half running, her face chalk white, looking only straight ahead. I didn't think she was seeing much. Her black hair was down on one side, and she wore her Chinese dress again. A long dress, narrow despite its slits. As I reached her near the elevator, she almost tripped on the confining skirt. I held her arm.

"Li?"

She looked up. "He . . . Claude . . ."

That was all she got out. People were watching. I got her into the elevator, and we rode up to the fourth floor. At her door, she fumbled in her bag. I took the bag, found her key, opened the door. Inside, she sat down on the edge of the couch. I closed the door. Her pale face was turned away, hidden by the loose black hair down on one side.

"He went toward the river," she said, talking to the far wall away from me. "Claude. He walked away from me."

"Trouble? The river?"

"I don't know. No, of course not."

"I should call the police."

She was silent. "No, let him be with himself. All these years of defeat he has never tried to die. He will not now."

"Unless something's changed," I said.

If she heard me, she gave no sign. "He was to be talked to for a job. A French company here. We walked together. A beautiful day, hot but beautiful. We had lunch outdoors, a small restaurant. We went to the French company. He would not go in. We stood there, and he would not go in. The people on the sidewalk pushed at us, walked around us. Claude turned from the building, walked toward the river. On a side street I begged him to return, talk to the French company. I cried. He said I should leave him, go home to Saigon, I was still young. I said that Saigon was not my home now, could never be. He said then I better find a home, go somewhere, find a man who was alive. He said he wanted to walk alone. He pushed me away when I tried to touch him, slapped me. He walked away from me. Toward the river."

"Why, Li? Has he done that before?"

She didn't answer, but she turned, looked toward me. Her small, perfect face was paler than ever. She got up and went into the bathroom. I heard water running. The hotel room was hot and silent with the yellow afternoon sun through the windows. I lit a cigarette and waited. If Claude Marais was going to the river for a reason, I should be calling the police. Sure or not. I didn't call the police. I smoked and waited in the sunny room.

The water in the bathroom stopped. Li Marais came out. Her black hair was down all around her small face, her skin was no longer pale as if she had freshened in cold water. There was no other change in her. She stood just outside the bathroom door, wearing the long, slim dress.

"Li?" I said. "Is Claude involved in some deal? Something illegal, maybe? Big enough for murder?"

"No."

"You're sure?"

"Yes. Dan? He walked away from me."

I said, "Can you be really sure what he's doing, Li?"

"No, perhaps I can't. I don't know. Dan—"

"Did he give something to Eugene, Li? Something Eugene was to hold for him? Something valuable, even dangerous?"

"Perhaps he did. Dan, he said I should find a man."

"What did he give Eugene, Li? What has he been doing?"

"There was a package. He sent it, I think. From the Congo," she said. She took a step toward me, one step. "He is not a husband to me. He won't touch me. Will you, Dan?"

It was her hotel room—and Claude's. "Here? Li, I—"

"Now," she said. "If you like me."

"Claude lives here too, Li. Any time he could come back."

She walked past me to the outer door, double-locked it, put on the chain. She stood with her back to the door.

"He would expect me to be here, he would not stop for a key at the desk. He would not knock. I might be asleep. He is a kind man. If he did guess, know, I think he wouldn't really care. Perhaps he would even approve."

"Do you want to get at him through me, Li?"

"I don't know. I want to be loved."

Claude Marais's wife and rooms. Wrong? No—not right and not wrong, only human. She had her need, so did I. Marty was gone. Some things just are, will be. Claude could walk in on us, but some risks must be, too. I kissed her at the door.

In her bedroom I found out what else she had done in the bathroom. When she took off the long dress, she had nothing on underneath.

Evening when I left, and she was asleep in the bed. She had cried the first time, and talked about all the places they had been, she and Claude, how good he had been then. The second time she cried and talked about herself and all she didn't understand that was pushing her into darkness. She talked about her childhood in Saigon when she had understood. After the second time, I was in love with her.

I didn't know if that was good or bad, and she fell asleep in the heat of the early evening, and I left. I knew that the bed had been good—for me and I hoped for her. I wasn't sure about the love or anything else, except that maybe the crying was good. Maybe she had needed the chance to cry and talk.

I knew I didn't really want to leave, but somewhere in my mind I was thinking of Claude Marais and the river. In the hotel room I had not thought about Claude or the river. Now I did, and I think I was going to walk to the river. Stupid. If he was in the river, I wouldn't find him. But he wasn't in the river.

As I went out into the heat of the street, I saw him coming toward the hotel at a distance. I stepped into a doorway until he had passed and turned into the hotel. He walked slowly, looked at no one. When I stepped out of that doorway I was still in love with Li Marais, but I did not feel good.

I had lost an afternoon of work. I had a murder to work on. Work is an answer.

14

Number 120 Fifth Avenue was a tall, older apartment house, its white stone façade gray with years of city grime. The apartment of Mr. Jules Rosenthal was on the tenth floor. The doorman told me that Mr. Rosenthal was away for the summer. I said I knew that, and took the elevator up. The doorman, after a good look at my clothes and missing arm, went to his house telephone.

The tall, military-looking man who had bumped me the night of Eugene Marais's murder was in the doorway of the apartment as I stepped off the elevator. He had that same haughty belligerence, and he recognized me. I saw that by a faint wavering in his stern eyes. He knew me, but I realized as I walked up to him that he wasn't quite sure where I knew me from.

"Hello," he said. He smiled.

The "hello," and the smile, told me a lot. He really couldn't place me, but he wasn't going to let me know that if he could help it. The style of a diplomat, or the trick of a salesman. The technique of a man who lived on contacts, sold his service not his skill, rose or fell not on what he knew, but on who he knew.

"Hello again, Mr. Manet," I said, not helping him.

His imperious bearing stiffened. I knew *his* name, and that gave me a big edge. He wasn't sure how I knew his name. It made him uneasy in his tailored dark blue suit. Blue was his color, it seemed—the color of the French military. The suit had the same military impression, as if he didn't want people to forget his martial reputation. In his lapel he wore a ribbon that I didn't know, but I was certain it was something better than the Legion of Honor.

"Well," he said, "come in, please."

Still trying not to reveal that he hadn't placed me in his mind. We went into a sumptuous sunken living room of deep yellow carpet and vast chairs, couches, tables and view of the city outside. I finally came to his rescue. After all, I wanted him to relax, to talk to me.

"My name's Dan Fortune, Mr. Manet. A private detective working on the Eugene Marais murder and robbery. The Balzac Union gave me your address. We bumped outside Marais's pawn shop a week or so ago, remember?"

His eyes remembered me now.

"Of course, I wasn't looking where I went," he said, regally taking the blame again. He looked solemn. "A tragic affair, poor Eugene. A stupid way to die. A cheap robbery."

"How do you know it was cheap?"

"The police have been to me, of course. Almost a week ago. I had not expected any further interrogation."

The police had dug Manet out *after* Jimmy had been arrested then. Part of their doubts.

"Things have changed," I said. "You knew Eugene Marais in Paris?"

"Our families were acquainted a long time ago. I, myself, did not know Eugene or Claude in those days."

"The hero days?"

"One did one's best, Mr. Fortune."

"Did Eugene Marais do his best then? In the Occupation?"

"In his way." He sat down now in a mammoth red womb chair, crossed his legs like a general being interviewed, indicated a chair for me to sit in. "Eugene was a quiet man, a shopkeeper. He was not a man to do much in action. Most men are like that, eh? The vast bulk of the world, the citizens."

"You met Eugene here through Claude Marais?"

"Yes."

"How did you meet Claude?"

"On business in San Francisco, Mr. Fortune. I represent many French companies abroad, public relations I suppose you would say. Claude Marais is quite different from Eugene, is well known in French circles. I considered that we would have mutual business interests, could cooperate."

"What business?"

"Wines, gourmet foods, perfumes, clothes."

"Two heroes for France?"

"If you like. I thought Claude could be an asset to some companies I represent. Unfortunately, when we met again here in New York, Claude thought otherwise."

"So you had a fight? At the Balzac Union?"

"He hit me, I do not brawl," Paul Manet said coldly. "Claude is a sick man, bitter against his own country, denying its truth and glory. He is no true Frenchman now. A shame."

"You're sure it wasn't a business fight? Some other business than wines or foods or perfumes?"

"I'm sure, Mr. Fortune."

"What did you talk to Eugene Marais about?"

"Paris, the past, the old times. Nostalgia, I suppose."

"Vel d'Hiv?"

"Perhaps it was mentioned."

"But you didn't like to talk about it?"

He thought a moment or two. "Do you know about Vel d'Hiv?"

"Yes. July 16, 1942. The roundup of Jews."

"Then you know why we don't like to talk about it. As a Frenchman, I am not proud of that night, or of what came after."

"But you were a hero, a fighter."

"I saved a few poor people, helped, resisted the Gestapo. To fight the Nazis then was not special heroism, a duty. No risk was too great, one did not have to decide much. All who could fought, helped. If I did more than many, I am happy, but it was long ago. Do you talk often of your past record, Mr. Fortune?"

"Not often," I said, "but I don't trade on it, either. I don't live off my reputation from the past."

I saw his anger again, quick and belligerent. Taller in the mammoth modern chair, menacing.

"Meaning that I do that?"

"You 'represent' French companies—only French, right? And 'represent' means you're a front man, a glad-hander, someone who gets respect for his employers not for how good their wares are, but for who and what he is. Did they hire you for your business knowledge, Manet, or for your heroic name? I'll bet you always live in apartments as plush as this one, and you never pay rent, right? A Jules Rosenthal everywhere to lend you his pad because you're a hero. A Balzac Union to roll out the red carpet for you. Not because you're really important, but because you were once a hero of France. A monument. A legend. I wonder what you'd be doing if you hadn't been a Resistance hero? Selling salami in some Paris shop? A factory hand?"

"You insult me, Mr. Fortune."

"Your military honor, Manet? When were you ever a soldier? You were a Resistance hero, a Maquis. Why the soldier act?"

Manet said, "Leave, Mr. Fortune, please. You are a cripple, I do not want to hurt you."

"Like you hurt Claude Marais? Maybe he didn't think you were a real soldier either. *He* was, right? Maybe that's what the fight was about. Or maybe he just didn't think much of a man still trading on his heroics of thirty years ago." I lit a cigarette, blew smoke into the palatial room. "If there were any heroics thirty years ago."

The silence that came down over the vast, expensive room was like the heavy, airless, yawning silence that comes in the hour before a hurricane explodes in all its fury.

"Did Eugene Marais know something about your past you never wanted anyone to know, Manet?" I said, smoked. "Facts about Paul Manet that would ruin his nice, soft existence?"

He took a deep breath, let it out. "You can check into the record of Paul Manet as far and as wide as you want, Fortune. You will find nothing hidden there."

"Maybe I'll have to do just that," I said. "Where were you the murder night, Manet? You left the pawn shop around five-fifteen in your car, where did you go the rest of the night?"

"For a drive, dinner at Le Cheval Blanc with businessmen, drinks with another businessman, and to bed here."

"What time did you leave that last businessman?"

"About eleven, I believe. Despite your image of me as a kind of business gigolo, I work very hard. I need my sleep on most nights."

"So you were alone after eleven P.M.? Or did you have an appointment with Eugene Marais at the pawn shop?"

"I was alone in my bed. Now you can—"

I heard a telephone receiver go down somewhere in the big apartment. Paul Manet wasn't alone. There were footsteps in the next room. Light steps, and the door opened. Naturally, I wasn't carrying my old gun. Luckily, I didn't need it. I saw a bedroom through the opened door, and Danielle Marais came out.

"Mr. Manet was my father's friend," the heavy, petulant girl said. "You can't accuse him."

"Was he a friend?" I said. "Or maybe only of Claude's, until they had a falling out?"

The long, dark hair of the dead Eugene's daughter was coiled up in a chignon, and she wore a new, green cocktail dress that had not come off some rack in Macy's. Her big, adolescent breasts stretched the sleek dress that was too old for her, too slim for her heavy body. But it did something for her, if you liked heavy, erotic nineteen-year-olds.

"You think Mr. Manet has to rob cheap pawn shops?" Danielle sneered. She wasn't a pleasant girl, but she was still young.

"There wasn't any robbery," I said. "It was a cover for the murder. They let Jimmy Sung go. Now they're looking for another motive. I think your father knew something Manet there didn't want known. Or maybe it was something else. Where'd you get that dress, Danielle?"

"From Charlie Burgos, of course," she snapped, and swung in a slow circle preening the new dress for me.

"Where did Charlie get that kind of money?"

"He works!"

"At his kind of pay that dress is a year's savings."

"What do you know?" she sneered, but she stopped giving me the show of her dress.

She stood in the room as if uneasy, a girl trying to be a woman and not making it. She seemed almost confused.

"What money does Charlie have, Danielle?" I said.

She chewed at her full lips, a habit she had probably found right after she stopped sucking her thumb. It was Paul Manet who answered me:

"I gave her the dress. Eugene Marais was a friend of mine, no matter what you think. I wanted to cheer Danielle up."

"A dress for a friend of the family?" I watched Danielle. She was grinning. "How long have you two known each other? Did Eugene and Viviane Marais know you knew each other? Maybe they didn't like it?"

"We only met after Dad was dead!" Danielle said hotly. "Mother thinks I'm a child, but I'm not a child anymore. See?"

She pulled her dress flat over her thighs and belly, outlined her body, and arched her back to show me her full breasts. It only showed what a child she was.

15

While I had the special veal cutlet at a diner on Sixteenth Street, I thought about the afternoon and Li Marais. I had tried not to think about her, or the afternoon, since I had left her asleep, and now I felt the hollow in the pit of my stomach. Was I in love with her? If I was, did it matter? Claude Marais had not gone into the river. He had probably done nothing, and she had been with him for eighteen hard years. I thought about something else. Not Marty.

I thought about how you checked the details of a man's actions thirty years ago in a foreign city under the rule of an invading army. Whatever had to be done, I couldn't do it. It was a police job. For all I knew, they might have done it, or be doing it, already. To be sure, when I finished my coffee, I walked to the precinct station. The hot spell was breaking. Masses of high black clouds moved in the last light over the city from New Jersey. We would get rain, and then it would cool for a time.

Lieutenant Marx was out of his office. Another detective said that Marx *had* contacted Paris about Paul Manet, but no word had come back yet. I left a message for Marx to call me—please.

Wind whipped up stray dust and a hail of paper in the street as I walked toward my office. The storm was blowing up fast. Thunder was rumbling across the now night sky as I reached my building on Twenty-eight Street, and the first heavy drops came down. By the time I got to my office door, the sky opened, and the torrent poured down the airshaft outside my open window. I hurried in to close my window, and the hands grabbed me.

At least four pairs of hands. A bag went over my head. I started to throw off the hands. Something poked into my back. A gun or a stick? I wasn't about to find out the hard way. I stopped struggling. A voice whispered close:

"Get him down, quick!"

I was walked, hustled, out of my door and down the stairs toward the street and the torrent of rain. I heard a lot of feet, and a lot of low, hard whispering. There was something familiar about it all—the grim guerrilla band. Kidnapping the important official. The bag over my head, the urgings to speed, the pell-mell flight down the stairs into the rain—like an IRA unit in action, the Brazilian political rebels. Too many newspapers, too many old movies.

I was soaked when they shoved me into a car. We drove off, drove for some time with the rain pounding on the roof of the car. An old car, the engine wheezing and the chassis creaking. A lot of turns around corners, right and left, and after a time I began to sense that we were driving around in circles, going a few blocks, then doubling back. Under the wet bag, I couldn't know whether they were circling to evade a tail, or just to try to confuse me, but I had a sudden hunch that when we stopped we would not be too far from my office.

We stopped. They pushed me out into the rain and an odd silence. All I could hear was the rain falling on something like thick grass or bushes, and cars hissing through the wet on some kind of highway. I was walked along some narrow path with an odor like hay, and down some narrow space between walls where the rain echoed in the night.

Then we were inside, the sound of the rain shut out and yet reverberating in a kind of emptiness. Footsteps on bare wood. Up stairs that creaked loosely. Two flights, and into a room on the third floor that smelled of stale cooking, musty plaster, and something burning. I was pushed down into a chair. The bag came off my head.

The first thing I saw were two candles burning in fruit-jar tops. They stood on orange crates, and were the only light in the long, dim-shadowed room. The windows of the room were covered by blankets, the heavy rain muffled outside in the night. I saw a long wooden table piled with empty cans, dirty dishes, and blackened Sterno cans. I saw mattresses on the bare floor, each mattress in a separated section with ragged clothes hanging on nails. The defined little areas like small rooms; one set of clean, sharp, gaudy dress clothes hanging in each section. I saw a television set all by itself along one bare wall like an idol on an altar. I saw four pale, unhealthy faces, and hungry, half-sane eyes, watching me from the candle-lit shadows. And I saw Charlie Burgos sitting on an orange crate in front of me.

"Why'd they let the Chinaman go, Fortune?" Charlie said.

"They found the stolen stuff, Jimmy Sung never had it. He's clear. Why, Charlie? Where do you fit?"

"I ask the questions, Fortune."

Too much TV, too many movies. The manner, the dialogue, of every tough guy who snarled his way through the cameras between commercials. With TV, anyone can know in an hour the way an FBI man, a Mafia soldier, or a Corsican bandit talks, looks, and acts. What no one can know from TV is why the Corsican acts as he does, how he got that way, what he feels inside. To know that is life, not television, and these kids did not know life beyond the slum streets and the hovels of their parents. An imitation, a surface ritual, that depended on the proper responses to maintain it. I wasn't about to play.

"Crap," I said. "You didn't rob the shop, Charlie. You wouldn't have dumped the loot. But you were at the shop that night. Why? Money? Some scheme? Did you give Eugene Marais too much? He could have hurt you? So you killed him?"

Charlie Burgos was up. "No way! I swear—!"

Automatic. This was real, an accusation. He had been accused all his life, and he reacted—protesting. Weak, a zero in the real world, and the weak can only protest, plead their innocence before power. Forgetting for the moment that in the dim room he was supposed to be the power, that he had me. The ritual lost for an instant. Then remembered, the script back.

"Back off, Fortune. You got nothing. We got you."

What else did the street kids know? What did they have to do with their time? A dreary past, a hungry present, and no future at all. Today would always be the same, unless it got worse, until they died. For one reason or another, for each of them this room was home. Parents who could give them nothing. Afraid of organizations, because, for them, all organizations turned into a man with a whip. Their only view of the bigger world from their depths was, like Gorky's bakers in their cellar, a single small window—the television set. They dealt with the bigger reality through the surface imitation of television, faced the tiger through its shadow.

I said, "Where do you fit, Charlie?"

"My business," he said, sat down. "The cops got any leads?"

"Ask them."

Another boy said, "We got you, we ask you, mister."

"Shut up," Charlie Burgos said, the boss. "The cops're nowhere. Maybe you got some ideas who killed the old man, Fortune?"

"You're worried, Charlie?"

"I got no worries. No problems at all."

"Danielle?" I said. "Maybe you know something about her? Her own father, you know?"

Charlie Burgos laughed. "Man, you're sure crazy."

"He didn't like you much, Charlie. Not for her."

"Hell, the old man was Jell-O, you know? No problem."

"How about Paul Manet?"

Charlie Burgos's face was bland. "What about him?"

"Manet and Danielle, maybe? Eugene Marais didn't like that? A fight, maybe? An accident? Maybe that's your interest in the thing, Danielle was dumping you for Paul Manet? You—"

"Danielle don't dump me for anyone. You're way off," the youth said, leaned toward me in the dim room. "Look, the old man was knocked over in a two-bit grab-and-run. Happens all the time in hock shops, right? Danielle and me we got plans, okay? She got to get something now the old man's dead. Only everyone's nosing around, and Danielle don't like that. You got her old lady paying you through the nose. That's money out of our pockets. For nothing. Whyn't you let the fuzz handle it, okay?"

"You beat me up, grab me, just because Mrs. Marais is paying me and that's lost money to you?"

"You're gettin' in the way." His voice was angry now. "Why the hell don't you leave town, take a vacation."

Was he needling me about Marty?

"I've got a job, I need money to eat, too."

"Okay, how much? How much to drop it, fade out?"

"I thought you figured I was taking money out of your pocket already."

One of the others said, "He's a hardhead, Charlie. Let's get rid of him."

"Yeh," one said.

"Permanent," a third added from the shadows.

It scared me. They were imitation tough guys, playing at an illusion, but they believed their own script, and if they followed it through all the way I'd be as dead as if they were a real gang of musclemen. They'd be caught, they weren't really strong, but that wouldn't help me. That they might kill me, I didn't doubt a second. They believed themselves. They had to. Alone in a big country that ignored their existence, alienated and forgotten, they had no chance and less hope. These boys had been given no hope, so they invented it—the hope of schemes, and plans, and big dreams of power and triumph.

I said, "Charlie, tell me what you know. I'll help you. Whatever you're doing, you'll get hurt unless—"

He broke in, cold. "I won't get hurt, mister. I'm on my way. Maybe you'll get hurt. Maybe the boys are—"

Only when I heard the car door slam below the dim room did I realize that the rain had stopped. The street boys heard the car door too. One of them went out of the room. He came back almost at once.

"Some guy parked in the alley. He's got a gun out!"

Charlie Burgos lifted the corner of the blanket covering a window, peered down. "It's that Kraut hanging around Danielle's uncle. What the hell does he want?"

They all crowded around Charlie Burgos at the window, whispering urgently. Like a pack of curious puppies. They were, after all, kids, most of them younger than Charlie Burgos. That had saved me in the alley when they attacked me, and it gave me my chance now. I walked to the door of the room, quick but softly, watching them. They didn't see me. I made the door and out.

I was almost down to the second floor when I heard them howl up in the room. Then I ran.

16

I came out of the building—an abandoned, crumbling, condemned brownstone, I saw now. I did not know where I was. The only unboarded door opened at the side of the brownstone into a narrow alley slick and cool with the rain. A narrow front yard was tall with brown weeds, wet in the night after the rain.

They would expect me to run to the street—the safety of a city man. So I ran left up the narrow alley and past a parked black car. At the rear corner of the condemned building I saw a shape, a face white in the night, a hand with a pistol.

"You, Fortune!"

I ran on into an open space behind the abandoned brownstone where two buildings had already been demolished leaving an emptiness in the city like a scar. I scrambled over the wet mounds of debris in the open space. The voice behind the pistol in the alley had been the ex-Legionnaire "associate" of Claude Marais—Gerd Exner.

I reached the far street. It was dark and deserted, the people not yet out again after the summer storm. I trotted left toward the wider avenue, no sound of running behind me. I didn't think they would come after me in the open when I was ready for them, but I watched the corner ahead in case they tried to head me off. There was no one at the corner. They probably didn't even know which way I had run. I looked back down the dark street toward the open space and the alley to be sure, and saw the black car turn out of the alley toward me.

I jumped into the cover of a doorway as the black car came to the corner, but the ex-Legionnaire, Gerd Exner, saw me. The car skidded to a stop, began to back up. Exner had a gun, I didn't, and I couldn't know what he wanted with me, or which side he was on. I ran up the wide avenue. The black car ground gears to come after me, the traffic on the avenue light in the dark after the storm.

I reached the next corner. The street sign high on its lamppost read: 10th Avenue—19th Street. I knew where I was. I ran left again down Nineteenth Street toward the condemned building where Charlie Burgos and his boys had taken me. Before the black car and Gerd Exner could follow, I jumped down into a sunken areaway in front of an Italian market. With any luck, Exner would think I was going back to the condemned building, and drive past me.

He did. The black car went on down the street toward the condemned building. It was all the break I needed. I knew where I was now, I'd gained a few moments, and Exner had lost sight of me.

I slipped along the dark streets back to my office.

This time no one was waiting for me in my office. I locked my door, just in case. Gerd Exner would know by now where my office was. All right, what did the ex-Legionnaire want? With me, or with Charlie Burgos, or both? What did Charlie Burgos want? With Charlie Burgos it was probably money. It was probably money with Gerd Exner too. Or was one of them a man who had killed, and who wanted me silent?

I heard the man coming up the stairs outside my office. He wasn't trying to be quiet. I got out my old cannon anyway, put it on my desk in plain sight. The man in the corridor could be going to some other office on my floor. A shuffling walk, like the furtive customers of the old men across the corridor with their funny pictures. But the old men wouldn't be open this late, so I watched my door.

The knob turned. I waited. A voice called out: "Mr. Fortune?"

Jimmy Sung's voice—sober, as far as I could tell. I got up and unlocked the door. Jimmy Sung came in. I checked the corridor. Jimmy seemed to be alone. I sat down at my desk. Jimmy Sung stood and looked at my big gun. He wasn't drunk the way he had been this morning, but he wasn't sober, either. A liquor shine to his eyes, a faint swagger to his stance, but not swaying or shaking. The alcoholic plateau, where, with a drink every so often, the alkie can function for hours as if perfectly sober. Maybe better.

"I went to the shop," Jimmy said, not slurring. "There was a package, you know? Like I said, maybe Mr. Marais was holding something for that Claude, and I remembered the package. In the safe. I remembered seeing it out the night Mr. Marais got killed. On a shelf in the back room."

"As if he was planning to give it to someone that night?"

"I don't know, but it ain't around the shop now."

"It wasn't on the list of what the robber took."

"It wasn't on no inventory, see? Just holding it."

"No idea what might have been in it, Jimmy?"

"Mr. Marais never said. I ain't even sure it was Claude's."

"Can you describe it?"

"Brown paper, waxed black string, about the shape of a shoe box. Mr. Marais's name was on the outside in black ink."

"It was addressed? You mean someone had mailed it to Mr. Marais? From where?"

"No, not mailed. No stamps. Hand-delivered, I guess. Kind of a label on it from some place in Africa, I think."

I reached for my telephone, dialed the number of the Hotel Stratford, asked for room 427. Li Marais's soft voice answered.

"Li? It's Dan."

A silence. Then her voice again, low, "Dan, no. I'll—"

"I have to talk to you now, Li."

"No, Dan, I cannot. Later, I will call you."

"Sorry, it's business, you understand. I'll come there."

"Claude is here!"

"Yeh," I said. "Don't run away on me, Li."

I hung up. "Let's go, Jimmy."

I didn't wait for the elevator. My clerk-friend said something I didn't hear as I went past, and Jimmy Sung was puffing when we reached the fourth floor and room 427. Claude Marais opened the suite door.

"Mr. Fortune?"

I went in past him, with Jimmy silent behind me. Claude Marais looked at Jimmy, then at me. Those slow, deliberate movements of his, as if even to bother to breathe was a wearying effort. For a moment, I wondered if he knew—about me, and Li, and the afternoon. There was something about his eyes. He said nothing, and I had more important matters to worry about.

Li was sitting in a far corner near the windows, almost hiding. She saw Jimmy, and smiled. It was a weak smile. She didn't smile at me. She and Claude weren't alone. Viviane Marais sat on a couch. It had all the look of an urgent family conference. The murdered Eugene's widow was out of her black, in a wine red dress that took ten years off her age. She was smoking, didn't rush to welcome me.

"You have something to talk about, Mr. Fortune?" Viviane Marais said.

"A lot. Jimmy's been cleared."

The widow nodded toward Jimmy Sung. "So I see. That was good work. You must give me your bill."

"When the work is finished," I said.

"Of course," she said. That was all. She smoked.

Claude Marais had come to stand near the widow. Somehow, they fitted better than Claude did with Li, small and Oriental in her corner. Or maybe that was my reflex prejudice.

I said, "You sent a package to Eugene, right, Claude?"

"No, I sent nothing."

"From the Congo. Size of a shoe box, brown paper. Eugene had it in his safe, I know that. You sent it, I know that."

Claude looked at me, and then, slowly, toward his wife in the far corner. Li Marais lowered her eyes. Claude shrugged.

"It was nothing important, African trinkets," he said. "A small pres-ent for Eugene."

"He wasn't holding it for you? You gave it to him?"

"Yes, of course."

"But he never opened it, right? You sent a small present all the way from the Congo, months ago, and Eugene just kept it in the safe unopened?"

Claude Marais said nothing. Li was still studying the floor under her tiny feet. I remembered those feet, small and bare. Viviane Marais watched us all like a perched hawk.

"Where's that package now, Claude?" I said. "It's not in the shop. It wasn't in the stolen loot."

"I don't know," Claude Marais said. "I don't care. I said, it is nothing of any importance."

"Maybe Gerd Exner knows where it is now," I said.

"No, Gerd has no interest in the package."

"He's got an interest in something," I said. "Something connected to you, Claude. He's still around. He's looking with a gun in his hand. He wants something, and he wants it bad. I think you have what he wants. I think your wife was right all along. Exner is dangerous, and you know it."

"No. Gerd is an old comrade, no problem. My wife made an error, nothing more," Claude Marais said. He seemed to think, sighed. "Gerd wishes me to join him in some work again, that is all. He attempts to persuade me. I am not interested."

True or a lie, Claude Marais was going to stick to his story. Without the package, or some other proof that he was lying, there wasn't much more I could say. There was nothing left to do but search this suite, turn it inside out, and if that uncovered nothing, look other places. I turned to Jimmy Sung to tell him to start searching. Viviane Marais was staring at her brother-in-law. Her sharp, alert eyes watched Claude. Her cigarette burned forgotten in her fingers.

"Mrs. Marais?" I said.

"That night," she said, still watching Claude. "The night Eugene died. He said Claude had been in the shop, Claude was supposed to come back. Eugene said Claude had to come back—to *get* something. Eugene had something of Claude's. Eugene said he was not sure Claude should have it. I remember. The last time Eugene called, I was half asleep. I forgot, thought only of the man he was waiting to meet, but now I remember."

Claude Marais said, "I was supposed to go back, but I didn't. We were going to talk about me going away from New York, going somewhere better for me. Getting the package wasn't necessary. I couldn't think of anywhere I wanted to go, so I didn't go to the shop. I went to bed, right, Li?"

"Yes," Li Marais said.

"You didn't stay in bed," I said. "You went to Gerd Exner, or called him, and you came to me. Where else did you go that night? What time did you leave the hotel again that night?"

"Exner called me. I went to you. Nowhere else," Claude said calmly. "I did not go to the shop."

I said, "Did Gerd Exner go to the shop?"

The outer door opened. We all heard it. One of those things. Someone, the last one in or Claude himself, had left it unlocked. Gerd Exner came into the suite. He had his gun out.

"No," Exner said. "I didn't go to the pawn shop."

17

Gerd Exner said, "Do I kill them, Claude?"

My gun was still in my office, not that it would have done me any good. He had his, I would have had to get mine out, and he was a soldier, a Legionnaire. He had the skill and the nerve, the experience of killing. He would be better, which is why I don't carry a gun unless I'm sure I need it for some specific reason. Someone, I've said before, is always better.

"No," Claude Marais said. "Put the gun away, Gerd."

"I came up unseen," Exner said. "You and Li can leave, be seen. I kill the three of them, no trace, we go back to our work. Yes?"

"We don't have any work to do anymore," Claude Marais said. "Hang up the guns, Gerd. The wars are over."

"The wars are never over," Gerd Exner said. His scarred face under the thin blond hair was like ivory. "You see it now? What do you do, Claude? How do you live? Like this, useless and rusting? It will not work, not for us. There is no way for us but what we know."

"There is no way for us at all," Claude Marais said. "All we can be is bandits. There is no purpose for us, nothing we can fight for anymore."

The tall ex-Legionnaire moved closer to Claude Marais, his limp more obvious now as if he had been running too hard. The gun in his hand remained steady, but there was a kind of anger in his pale blue German eyes. He spoke only to Claude, but he did not relax his watch.

"Purpose?" Exner said. "What do we wish with purposes, Claude? Causes? Patriotics? Those things are for amateurs and fools. We are soldiers, nothing else. We fought for nations and purposes, for France, and France failed us. All nations fail their soldiers. A man cannot put his trust in nations or politicians. We must trust only ourselves, fight only for ourselves. Mercenaries, Claude. Both of us."

Claude Marais shrugged. "Perhaps for you, Gerd, but it is not so for me. I do not want to fight. I told you so."

In her corner, Li Marais stood up suddenly. Her small, full body was shaking under the Chinese dress. I found myself wondering if she had anything on underneath the dress now. Her gentle, rigid face was agitated, no longer calm.

"Go away," she said to Gerd Exner. "Go away from Claude, please. Leave us alone, Exner!"

The German mercenary seemed to think about it, watched Li Marais speculatively. "You hired this detective here to scare me away, told him lies. Now you ask me to leave Claude alone. You like him as he now is? A shadow man?"

"No," Li Marais said, "but I do not want him like you, a jackal preying on everyone."

"So? I see what has been done to Claude," Gerd Exner said. "Women can ruin a man. You have destroyed a good soldier. I have seen it before. Aryan women are strong, they inspire a man to conquer, but you gook women are weak, you do not understand a white man. You weaken him, ruin him."

Claude Marais moved, stepped at Exner. The tall German with the scarred face backed away, his gun up and aimed at Claude. The quick, animal reaction of a wary professional gunman in his blue eyes. He would shoot on an instant, as much from fear as from intent. To shoot at any possible threat was how a mercenary survived. Claude Marais knew this, stopped.

"No more, Gerd. Get out of here now. Get out of this city, this country. We have nothing together. You're nothing more now than a hired killer!"

"So?" Exner said again, considered Claude Marais. "Very well, you are useless now, anyway. I'll go, but first I think I will take that package the detective there is looking so hard for, eh? It is half mine, but now I think it should be all mine, yes. Where is it, Claude?"

"I don't know."

Exner smiled. "Come, this is Gerd you talk to, eh? It is not found, I know that from the detective. Who else would have a package of Claude Marais's?"

"I don't know who has it, or where it is," Claude Marais said. "If I find it, I'll send it to you. If there is anywhere you can stay long enough to receive mail, Gerd."

The click was like a slap in all our faces. Gerd Exner had cocked his pistol. It was aimed at Claude Marais.

"You're lying, Claude. I think I will have to kill you too. All of you. I—"

The shape, figure, man, seemed to come from nowhere. Out of the air of the hotel room. Suddenly there, a shape jumping at Gerd Exner with a wild, unintelligible cry of rage. Exner half turned to face the shock—a shock as much psychological as physical. Surprised, stunned, his gun slow in turning.

Perhaps it was that Exner was getting older. Maybe that he was in New York, and not as alert, wary, as normal. Perhaps only the arrogance of years of sneering at the "gooks," ignoring them as human beings, despising them as weak. After a time, not even seeing them at all.

Exner had forgotten Jimmy Sung. I suppose we all had. Away against a wall, silent, taking no part, everyone had forgotten that Jimmy Sung was even in the room. Until, wildly, Jimmy Sung charged, and Exner turned too slowly.

Exner shot.

I saw blood on Jimmy Sung's arm. It didn't stop him. Half crazy, half drunk, he crashed into Gerd Exner. The tall German staggered, almost fell, held on to a table. It was my chance. I grabbed his gun arm from behind, twisted with all I had. Exner cried out, the gun dropped.

I held on.

Jimmy Sung punched Exner in the face. Viviane Marais had a heavy ashtray, swung it at Exner, missed.

Li Marais scrambled on the floor, got the pistol. She held it in both hands, aimed at the German, still cocked. Exner stopped fighting. Jimmy sat down on the floor, held his arm.

I took the gun, picked up the telephone, told George Jenkins down at the desk to get the police.

Claude Marais stood alone where he had been. He had not moved. Passive, he watched as if none of it concerned him. As I hung up the receiver, Claude Marais lit a cigarette.

18

Three uniformed patrolmen and an ambulance doctor arrived at the suite first. The patrolmen took charge of Gerd Exner and his gun, and the ambulance doctor worked on Jimmy Sung. Jimmy had taken a shot through his right upper arm—a clean wound that had hit no bone or major blood vessel. The police listened to the story, gave Jimmy Sung nods of solemn admiration. They lived with daily danger, admired bravery.

"Nice work, mister," one patrolman said.

"He threatened three of you," another patrolman said, writing laboriously in his report book, "wanted Mr. Marais there to go with him on some work. When Mr. Marais refused, he then threatened to shoot you all, and Mr. Sung stopped him. That it?"

"More or less," I said.

"What's this about some package?"

"Exner seemed to think Marais had a package that was half his, said he wanted all of it," I said.

Claude Marais said, "I have no package. It was unimportant. Some trinkets."

The patrolmen nodded. One made his notes, and that was all. The package wasn't their problem. When the ambulance doctor had finished with Jimmy Sung, he left. The rest of us waited. Gerd Exner had said nothing since the police had arrived, sat silent with two patrolmen beside him. Jimmy Sung lay on the couch, his arm bandaged, shaking now that the moment of action was over. Claude Marais smoked, still stood where he had the whole time. Li Marais had gone back to her chair in the corner. Viviane Marais was smoking too. I just waited.

Lieutenant Marx and two other detectives showed up half an hour later. Marx listened to the patrolman's report, made me tell it all again, nodded approval of Jimmy Sung's crazy attack, considered Gerd Exner and Claude Marais. He watched them, but he spoke to me.

"We got the report from Paris on Paul Manet, Dan," Marx said. "He's everything he says. Saved ten Jews that night in 1942 by hiding them, then rescued three others right out from under the Gestapo's nose. Went on to build quite an Underground record after that. Since the war he's absolutely clean. He represents ten French companies all over the world, lives high, but has no record and no hint of any illegal activity."

I didn't know why Marx was bringing up Paul Manet then, but he had to have a reason. He'd tell me when he was ready, or it would show soon enough.

"We'll take Exner," Marx went on. "We've been watching him. He's in the country illegally in the first place. Had to come in like that, he's wanted in half a dozen countries, not to mention Interpol. A little something about opium trading and all that. The D.A. and Washington are going to have a field day on the extradition. After we get finished with what we've got here."

Gerd Exner shrugged, his blue eyes already calculating what chances he had, what angles he could work on. Marx turned his attention to Claude Marais. I became aware of something missing. The other two detectives who had come in with Lieutenant Marx seemed to have vanished. I hadn't seen them leave the suite. Marx studied Claude Marais for a moment.

"Interpol is interested in Marais there, too," the Lieutenant said. "No specific charge, though. Some countries want him, but it's for gun-running, political action, that kind of stuff. No crimes straight out, except maybe one little matter. That right, Mr. Marais?"

Claude Marais smoked. "You are the one talking, Lieutenant."

"So I am," Marx said. "You don't want to tell us about a batch of diamonds? Seems they turned up missing down in the Congo a while back, just when you and Exner there were making a deal for guns with some rebel group. Those rebels were pretty mad. They say the guns turned out no good, and the diamonds did a vanishing act. So did you and Exner. You didn't carry the stones out, customs is sure of that. Now I'm hearing all this talk of some package."

Claude Marais said nothing. He smoked. Li Marais was up straight in her chair, watching him. Viviane Marais was staring at Claude too. On the couch, Jimmy Sung made a sound. Lieutenant Marx ignored Jimmy.

"You smuggled a package to Eugene, right? He had it in his safe, Jimmy Sung there saw it. Mrs. Marais says he mentioned returning something to you the night he was killed. Jimmy says he saw the package out of the safe that night late, on a shelf in the back room. Now we didn't find any package, did we?"

"I would not know, Lieutenant," Claude Marais said, his voice wary. "I have not seen the package since before Eugene was murdered."

"No? That's funny. It's funny, too, that you say it's not important, no value, just trinkets."

"All right," Claude said, "it is diamonds. I did send it to Eugene to hold for me, it is half Exner's. It is worth much money, but I am not interested in money. I planned to get it from Eugene that night, yes. I planned to give it all to Exner. I want no part of it. But I did not return to the shop that night, I have no idea where it is."

"Why didn't you tell us about it? A fortune in diamonds there in the shop, your brother murdered, the fortune missing, and you didn't mention it?"

"I thought—" Claude shrugged again, stopped.

"Thought what?" Marx said. "That Gerd Exner had taken the diamonds and killed your brother? Why protect Exner? You say you want no more to do with Exner."

"I . . . Gerd was an old comrade. Eugene was dead. I could not help Eugene. If Gerd killed him it was by chance, an accident when Eugene refused to give him the package. It would not help Eugene to tell, and I could not inform on Gerd."

"No," Marx said, shook his head. "Pretty, but no. You were silent because you wanted that package. We had a tip that the package is right here. Exner didn't kill Eugene, at least not alone. You were in the shop that night, and you have the package. Is that right, Sergeant?"

Marx spoke to the doorway into the suite bedroom. One of his detectives stood there. The detective held a shoe-box-sized package wrapped in brown paper and string.

"Inside the heat register, Lieutenant," the detective said. "Cover taken off, the package shoved in, cover screwed back."

"A tip?" I said.

"Anonymous, of course," Marx said. "The package we wanted was here, it said. Disguised voice. We didn't know about the package. We questioned. A package taken from the pawn shop, the tipster said, that night. Could have been man or woman. We sat on it, took it slow, then your call came about the trouble here, Dan. It fitted nicely."

"I took no package," Claude Marais said. "Put it nowhere."

Jimmy Sung sat up on the couch. Li Marais was on her feet, took a step toward Claude. Viviane Marais swore.

"Eugene wouldn't give you the package!" the widow cried.

Li Marais said, "Claude?"

"You were out that night, you came to me," I said.

Lieutenant Marx had the package open. He poured a little mound of glittering, gem-cut diamonds onto a table.

"There's a motive anyone understands," Marx said.

Gerd Exner said, "You swine, Claude! Idiot!"

Exner laughed then, and Jimmy Sung stood in the doorway to the bedroom. He held a small metal object—metal and enamel.

"I looked into the register," Jimmy Sung said. "This was back inside. He killed Mr. Marais."

Jimmy Sung lunged toward Claude Marais, bandaged arm and all. Two patrolmen stopped him. Lieutenant Marx took the metal object. I looked at it. It was a military hat badge, the kind worn on berets. A French hat badge.

"Could it have just fallen into the register?" Marx said.

"No, too big," the detective who had found the package said.

"Is it his?" Marx asked Li Marais.

Li Marais looked at it, and at Claude. "Oh, Claude!"

Claude Marais stared at his wife. Then he lit another cigarette.

19

I was tired, but I didn't want to go home or be alone. Sometimes it's like that when a case ends.

Claude Marais said nothing more to anyone. It wasn't the time to talk to Li, not about anything. I'm not sure I wanted to talk to her then. She went with Claude and the police, and Viviane Marais went home to Sheepshead Bay. When I asked the widow if she was satisfied, she looked at me for some time, then said we would talk tomorrow, or in a few days.

I went to the Black Lion where my old friend and bartender, Joe Harris, was working. I told him the whole story.

"Sounds like he did it," Joe said. "Simple motive."

An ex-soldier with a shadowy past sends a fortune in diamonds to his quiet brother. The brother wants him to settle down to normal work, so refuses to hand back the diamonds. There's an argument, made desperate by Gerd Exner being around, and the quiet brother is killed. All the rest is Claude trying to make it look like simple robbery. Motive—the diamonds. Opportunity—Claude was expected at the shop, I proved he had been out that night late. But . . . ?

"Who tipped the cops," I said to Joe. "Why and how?"

"Someone who hated him, someone who was afraid of him, or maybe someone who just wanted to get rid of him. Who knows how the tipster knew the stuff was there?"

"The tipster could have planted the diamonds there for any of those reasons, too," I said. "And that hat badge."

Anyone would fit. Charlie Burgos? For Danielle, maybe? Had Charlie seen Claude that night, and that was his interest in the affair?

Protecting someone—first by trying to stop me, then with a frame-up? Li Marais? The way Claude had looked at her. Maybe Claude had done it, and she had turned him in—for me? Maybe Claude knew that? His silence?

It was after midnight when I went home. I had a bad taste in my mouth. It all fitted, and yet . . . ? I swore at myself as I opened my apartment door, and stopped. Listened.

Someone was in the apartment. I knew it, sensed it. I barely breathed just inside the door in my dark living room, and looked down at the outer door lock. It hadn't been touched. Yet I knew someone was inside, waiting somewhere in my five rooms.

I breathed lightly, didn't move. As my eyes became accustomed to the dark in the living room, I saw nothing. Except that my bedroom door was closed. I never closed it, not in the heat of a New York summer, and this morning it had not yet rained and cooled the city. I took off my shoes, laid them carefully down, stepped softly into the kitchen and found a butcher knife on the counter. I reached the bedroom door without a sound, and listened. There was a faint line of light under the door. Someone had my small bedside reading lamp on—the low bulb.

My lone hand shook, but I held the knife and opened the bedroom door at the same time. I opened the door fast, jumped inside and left.

"Hello, Dan," Marty said.

She was in bed. The reading light on, shaded and turned low, but she wasn't reading. She was watching me, the strange contrast of her almost boyish face and woman's body never more sharp. The smile, and the soft, almost velvet eyes. I closed the door, put the knife on a table, went to her.

"I got back tonight," she said. "Come to bed. Now."

I didn't kiss her, I don't know why. Something about her, about her there waiting in my bed. A decision. I undressed, but I didn't get into bed. I sat on the bed.

"How was the vacation?" I said.

"Fine," she said. "Dan? We can talk later."

"I've just finished the Marais killing. It was the brother," I said. I told her all about it, step by step. The whole case, except Li Marais. I talked because her eyes told me she wasn't interested. No, she didn't want to hear the story, so I told all of it to keep from knowing what she had to talk about.

"Dan?" she said. "Don't you want to?"

"I want to," I said. "Tell me what it is, Marty."

She looked down, but only for a second. "I'm getting married. Next week."

I'd known, in a way, but knowing and being sure are not the same. To *know* a man is a murderer, and to be *sure* of it, aren't the same at all.

"Who?" I said. We always want to know that, we men. Who? Is he better than I? Richer, nicer, gentler, better in bed? It isn't going to be easy to liberate the men.

"Kurt Reston," she said.

The director, the theater man. The other man who had long believed in her work, in her. But a man going places, who still believed in winning the same prize she wanted.

"I can't go on drifting, Dan," she said. "Day to day where the wind blows us. He can give me what I have to have."

"We all drift. In the end, that's all we really do."

"No," she said. "There has to be more. More than waking up each morning and wondering what's going to happen today. I want to know what today's going to be like. Real things, solid. A base to start from, no more empty space when I'm not working. An anchor to stop the drifting."

"Marty, there isn't any anchor except to fill our time with as much sun as we can. You know the old Coverdale Bible? 'Let us leave some token of our pleasure in every place, for that is our portion, else we get nothing.' Marty—"

"No!" She sat up in the bed. I looked away. She was near to crying. "Maybe you're right, Dan, but I know now that I can't leave pleasure in every place. I want one sure place, and the sure pleasures. I want the rewards of this life, here and now, the way it is. With you I'd drift on and on without tomorrow. Two castaways in a lifeboat."

"And you want the ship, the ocean liner."

"Yes. First class."

"It's a ghost, the ship. A Flying Dutchman."

"Maybe, but you can see it. People know it's there. They see it, wave to it. No one sees your lifeboat down in the high waves alone."

She wanted to be seen, waved to. Wanted her existence testified to by the eyes of others. So that she'd know that maybe she did really exist after all. The normal need.

"They'll see you, Marty," I said. I smiled. After all, I'd been with this woman for a long time.

"Come to bed," she said. "Once more, Dan. For us."

"I don't think so," I said. "No."

I wanted to, yes, then why did I say no? Because it would make it harder? No. To hurt her, to attack her. Deny myself, refuse her, not let her be nice to me. Make her guilty so I could feel better. People are made of that irrationality.

She got up and dressed. When she was dressed, I wanted her back in bed even more. I'm as irrational as the next person.

"Will you be all right?" she said.

"I'll be fine."

"I'll . . . I'll call you."

"Sure," I said.

She went out of the bedroom, and out of the apartment. Out of my life. I lay down, and closed my eyes.

They began, the thoughts. The plans for revenge, the schemes of victory. The scenes where I stopped her, where I appeared at the wedding to stand between her and him, and she came to me. The dreams where she ran to me, and we were married, and lived in a big house and . . .

I was dressed, and on the cool night streets. Walking. Uptown, that's where a Kurt Reston, director, would live. On my way to find his house, his pad, to show her how much more of a man I was. Take her away. All our years had to mean . . .

I was in a bar. Naturally. What else does a man do when his woman has gone? He gets drunk, of course. Very drunk. He gets drunk and laughs with strangers and watches late-night TV above the bar and tells war stories. Strangers are very nice people in bars, and they are interested in how I lost my arm. First the arm, then the woman, then . . .

Claude Marais was a drifter. Do drifters kill? Not their brothers. Drifters don't have brothers. Of course they kill, especially their brothers. And wives . . .

Sun. Cool. Daytime taverns are oddly quiet and cool and dim. Lazy, a sense of endless time . . .

Dark. I'm glad you asked how I lost my arm. It's a long story. The war, you know? We were up near the Meuse River, that's in France, and this Tiger tank came. I saw its shadow in the fast water, the shadow of the Tiger. So, I had the shadow of a bazooka, and I shot that Flying Dutchman . . .

Roaches on a ceiling don't like the sunlight, their thin feelers quiver uneasy . . .

She had a nice face above her glass, blonde and raped at fourteen by some uncle her father beat her for enticing. Old, at fourteen. Come on, Dan, honey, I've got a nice place and we can talk. Fourteen is getting old in Saigon. I don't know anything about Saigon, I'm studying to be an artist. I never saw a man with one arm so close . . . honey . . .

Sure Claude Marais did it. What else? Only no one saw him, did they? No one saw Eugene Marais refuse to give him that package. No witnesses. She had a nice face, old and dark-haired, and where the hell was I now . . . ?

The Oriental women are so small in the dark.

20

A familiar room, and hot. Too hot. The hot spell had broken, then why was it so hot? And if I was in my own familiar room with Marty in bed beside me, asleep and small, then . . . ? In bed with me? Marty? I touched her, kissed her.

Li Marais looked up at me, sleepy but waking fast, not smiling as I touched her. "How are you, Dan?"

I lay back on the pillow. "Tell me. How did I get here?"

A familiar room, but not my room. The bedroom of the suite in the Hotel Stratford. Soft sun, so morning, and too hot.

"How long have I been?" I said.

"Only since last night, Dan. You came here with me last night. I found you in a bar," Li said, watched me.

"No, I mean how long since—?" I was going to say since Marty left me. I said, "Since they arrested Claude?"

"A week," Li said. "One more day."

That explained the heat—another hot spell on the city. I had missed the relief. A drunk binge. Booze, and how many strange women? The standard answer for a middle-aged roustabout. One week and a day, the exact time. She would be married, Marty. All over. My subconscious planned well, with precision. The next step: pack a bag and go. Or work?

"Claude's still in jail?" I said. "Nothing new?"

"He is in jail. There is nothing new. The French Consul, the Balzac Club, they are helping. I have engaged the lawyer, Kandinsky. They have not made a full charge, but he is in jail."

"You found me in a bar? For me, or for him?"

"For him, and for me," Li said. "Not for you. For myself, I was so alone. I found you."

I sat up, lit a cigarette. "I make you happy, Li? Even drunk? Did I tell you why I was drunk?"

"You make me happy. You told me, yes. I am sorry."

"If I make you happy, what do we care about Claude?" I made it brutal. To find out. Or was I feeling brutal?

She didn't flinch. "Eighteen years I have loved Claude. He does not love me now, loves nothing. But he is innocent. He could not kill Eugene. He did not want the diamonds. He would have given them to Gerd Exner, there was no hurry, he did not go back to the pawn shop that night. After all our years across the world we came here, and Claude found Eugene. He found for Eugene an admiration, yes. What in the past had been bad in Eugene, Claude now saw was good. A simple man who knew life and did what he could without need of credit, or glory, or purpose. An honest man enduring his obligation to live. That is what Claude said of Eugene. Would he kill Eugene for diamonds?"

"He was going to give Gerd Exner the diamonds? All of them? Break with Exner?"

"Yes, I know that. I was afraid of Exner, I hired you, but I was wrong. Claude was not returning to our past life."

"How do you prove it, and did Exner know it?"

"I don't know."

Under the thin sheet she was small, slim, but not thin. A full woman. Mine? Stay, pack no bag? How did I know?

"The police have all the circumstances against Claude. No more than that. But we have nothing, either. Empty time where Claude was alone. How do we prove him innocent, Li?"

"He did not go back that night. He was here, with me," she said. "The police do not believe me."

"What time, Li?"

"From nine-thirty until past three A.M."

"Not good enough."

"Eugene would not have waited until past three A.M. If he had been alive by then, he would have gone home."

I believed that. Even the police would agree, but how did we know Claude had been with her until 3:00 A.M. The wife? No, the police could not believe her. Did I?

"All right, say Claude is innocent. Who got the package from the shop after Jimmy Sung left, and who put it in this suite? Why? Not Exner, he wouldn't give up the diamonds. Who would give up a fortune just to frame Claude?"

"To escape capture for murder, Dan, what are diamonds?"

It was a good point. "What about that hat badge? How would someone get it? Was this room burglarized, broken into?"

I didn't add that one person could easily have gotten the badge and put it into the register—her.

"No, no one came here that I know of. No signs of entry."

She could have said yes, covered herself.

"Someone tipped the police to look here for the package," I said. "Maybe Claude is innocent, maybe he's guilty. I'll try to find out—for you. Don't use me, Li. Don't play with me."

She was silent. Then she moved under the sheet, touched her own body. "We are we. I must save Claude, he did not hurt Eugene. I must free him, but he does not need me. In jail he does not care, he smiles. He is alone. I need you, Dan, but I must help him. Then—?"

She kissed me. It was a real kiss. But, of course, I was thinking of myself.

Lieutenant Marx watched us as we sat down. Li perched on the hard chair in the squad room office. I faced Marx. He must have known about Marty, the police don't miss much, but he said nothing.

"When do you charge Claude Marais?" I said.

"You too?" Marx scowled. "That lawyer, Kandinsky, is on our backs every hour. Not to mention the French people." He looked at Li. "The little lady is persuasive."

"She knows Claude didn't do it," I said.

"I wish I did," Marx said, angry and yet not. "Even if we believed her, the time doesn't help. He could have killed his brother any time between three A.M. and five A.M."

"Would Eugene have waited until three A.M. in the shop?"

"We thought of that. But what kind of proof is it? Any man could have a million reasons for waiting, damn it."

I heard an odd uneasiness in the Lieutenant's voice. That wasn't like the police. An obvious uncertainty, as if they weren't really convinced of their own case against Claude. That they would be uncertain wasn't so unusual, but that Marx would show it to me was. It had to mean trouble in holding Claude.

"If only Marais would say something we could work on," Marx said, glared at Li. "He just denies it all, can't account for his time between three and when he went to you, Dan. He won't account for it. Walking around, he says, a habit. Gerd Exner had called him, and he was wondering who you were, deciding what to do about you."

"But you haven't charged him?"

"No. We're holding him as a material witness for now."

"For how long, Marx?"

"Not too long unless we get something more."

"What can you get? All right, circumstantially he looks like it, but no one can place him at the shop, no one saw Eugene killed, no one can even say Eugene refused the package and that there was a fight."

"We're looking," Marx said.

"Are you looking for that tipster?"

"An anonymous phone call in this city? How?"

"It has to be someone connected, someone with a motive to expose Claude Marais, or to frame him."

"We don't even know if it was a man or a woman."

"Maybe we better find out," I said.

Marx said nothing. He just looked gloomy.

21

I stopped at my office for my old gun, and walked with Li Marais to the condemned brownstone on Nineteenth Street where Charlie Burgos and his street kids had taken me. The yard was overgrown with sickly city weeds. The alley beside the house was deserted. Li Marais looked up at the dark, boarded windows.

"Someone lives here?"

"Street kids," I said. "If they have homes, they hate them, and where else can they get a place of their own?"

"You think this Charlie Burgos can help us?"

"I think he knows something."

We went up warily. As we reached the third floor, I had my pistol out. If Charlie Burgos could tell us anything, we weren't going to learn what this time. The third floor room where I had been held was empty. Not abandoned, the clothes, mattresses and blackened Sterno cans still there.

I searched the ragged belongings of the five adolescents. It took only a few minutes, they had so little. I didn't have much more of my own, but for me it had been a matter of choice to live without baggage. The street boys had never had a choice.

On the street I found a telephone booth. Li Marais waited on the hot sidewalk while I called Viviane Marais. People who are unaware of being observed reflect in their pose, their faces, the hidden skeleton of their feelings. Relaxed for an instant, they reveal the landscape where their minds are living. While the telephone rang out in Sheepshead Bay, I watched Li outside the booth. She watched the street and two children playing. Her Oriental face was blank, serene, as if she wasn't there at all.

"Yes?" Viviane Marais said from the other end.

"Dan Fortune, Mrs. Marais. Is Danielle there?"

"No." A silence. "I owe you some money, Mr. Fortune."

"Where is Danielle?"

"I do not know. She has not been home for two days. With that boy, I presume." Another silence. "You still work?"

"Li thinks Claude didn't do it."

"And what do you think?"

"I want to talk to Danielle and Charlie Burgos."

"I have not seen them."

"Do you still think Claude killed Eugene?"

"For a package of diamonds?" A third silence. "Or because Eugene interfered? What does it matter? I do not really care anymore. Send me your bill, Mr. Fortune."

She hung up. I went out to Li Marais.

Paul Manet walked back into the sumptuous living room of his borrowed apartment. I closed the outer door, followed him across the yellow carpet. Li Marais was silent behind me. Manet held a drink. He drank, composed his face into a somber expression.

"So Claude killed his brother? A tragedy. But—?" He sighed, drank. "We knew that Claude was disturbed."

"Li, there, doesn't think Claude did it."

"Li?" Manet looked at her. I saw the appreciation in his eyes. He squared his shoulders ready to be charming, gallant, and, hopefully, something more?

"Claude's wife," I said. "You didn't know that?"

"Ah, no," Manet said, very sad. "My sympathies, Madame."

The tall hero was out of his elegant, pseudo-military clothes. A dark shirt and tapered slacks like an officer at ease in his quarters. A looseness to his imperious manner, off-duty. Almost sluggish, but not relaxed. A tension in his face. Drinking. Was it that no one could keep the front up all the time? The need of a few drinks every afternoon before he went out to perform? I knew fifty salesmen like that. Yet with Manet it was something more. A pervading sense of need to have the drinks, a desperation.

"We're looking for Danielle Marais," I said.

"I have not seen her for some days."

"Charlie Burgos?"

"No, not him, either."

His eyes flickered. He had realized that he had just told me something I hadn't known for sure. He did know Charlie Burgos. He drank.

"So you know Charlie Burgos?" I said.

"I have met him with Danielle, yes."

"But you give Danielle dresses?"

"The daughter of a friend."

"No romance?"

"At my age?" He smiled. A weak smile.

"She was here alone that day. Why?"

"Why not? I am a family friend." He put down his drink. "Mr. Fortune, I am aware the police inquired into my history. I assume they told you what they found. I have nothing to hide. So, if you don't mind, I have an appointment."

Smooth, controlled, even commanding—and yet there was the tension. Everything in the elegant living room was a hair off. As if just out of focus.

"Someone was supposed to meet Eugene Marais the night he died. It almost had to be you, Manet. Why?"

"You saw me leave at five. I did not return."

"Why would you meet with a man from the past so late at night and alone? A man *you* hadn't really known at all before? A man who had known not you but your family in Paris."

Manet put down his drink. "I am becoming annoyed."

"Where do Charlie Burgos and Danielle fit in?" I pushed on. "They were there, so . . . *There*, sure! That's it. They *saw* you come out of the shop carrying a suitcase—and the diamonds?"

"There are laws to stop you badgering a—"

"Wait. You ditched the suitcase, but you kept the diamonds. You know where Claude Marais lives. You know the hat badge of the Thirteenth Half Brigade—his unit. But why? What did Eugene Marais do, or know, that—?"

"Get out! Now!"

His hands clenched into fists. Anger flushed his handsome face. He took a step toward me, powerful and commanding. I reacted by reflex.

I fell into a crouch with my lone fist raised. In a fight, I wouldn't have much chance with Manet, but a man reacts by instinct. To protect himself, or to attack.

I didn't do either. I didn't have to.

Paul Manet stopped. Instantly. He jerked back from my crouch and one fist. His reflex—the flinch again. When opposed, challenged, he broke. The haughty, belligerent manner broke apart. For the blink of an eye Manet almost cringed.

All at once I knew—Paul Manet was a fake.

The commanding manner was learned. The haughtiness built, assumed. The aristocratic assurance a mask. A fake.

Yet, his past and reputation was open and certain. His heroism was certified, a part of history. His heroic moment. Moment? *One* moment?

Was that it? A man who had once risen to a moment that was not really in his nature? A moment beyond himself—and he knew that inside? Ever since he had been faking the stance of that one moment, living on it when he knew inside that it was false? Beyond one moment built on special circumstances, he was no hero at all, but needed the rewards his "heroism" had brought, so went on playing the role even long after he himself knew it was fake, nothing was there inside?

"Come on," I said to Li Marais.

We left him standing there alone, not touching his drink on the table, his eyes as blank as the eyes of a blind man. He wouldn't tell me whatever the truth was, but if I was right, he would be afraid. He would worry, and maybe make a mistake.

22

We caught a taxi. "Did Claude mention Paul Manet, Li?"

She sat close against me. "Only that he came to Claude with a business offer. Claude was not interested."

"This was in San Francisco?"

"Yes. Later, Manet came here, but Claude disliked him."

"Yet Manet used Claude as an intro at the Balzac Union. He met Eugene, and . . . No, he didn't meet Eugene at the Union. He met Eugene outside." I thought as we rode downtown. We were near Li's hotel. "I want to talk to Claude. We'll call Lieutenant Marx from your hotel suite."

She opened her suite door, pointed to where the telephone stood. I didn't look at the telephone. Claude Marais sat in an easy chair facing us. Li glanced at the bedroom. A giveaway glance. Did it matter? Two used pillows on the unmade bed. Claude knew, had to know.

"They let me go. The lawyer got a paper, something," he said. "Are you all right, Li?"

"Yes. Mr. Fortune is helping me prove you innocent."

"How is he doing that?"

I said, "Are you innocent?"

"Who is?" That sleepwalking smile of his. "But prove it for Li, yes? For me, too."

"I want to know about Paul Manet."

Claude shook his head. "Not him, no. He leaves a bad taste. I'm not sure why. I suppose I leave a bad taste for many, eh? The used hero, the duped pawn. Like those honest, eager, very brave secret agents they used during World War Two for nothing except to be caught and die. A level of poor fools to give to the Germans, so that underneath them, really hidden, real agents did their work. A filthy world."

"How did you meet Paul Manet?"

"He came to me in San Francisco, wanted me to work for his companies. Another propagandist for wine and perfume at high prices. I turned him down, but he came here, too. I couldn't stomach him anymore, we fought."

"But he looked you up in San Francisco? Did you know him?"

"I'd heard of him. Most Parisians have."

"Did you introduce him to people there?"

"A few. He wanted introductions."

"To Eugene here, too?"

"No, he never asked to meet Eugene. Somehow he even missed Eugene at the Balzac Union. They met by chance up here one day. Manet had come to try to gloss over our fight. I didn't want to gloss it over."

"How did Eugene act?"

"Act?" Claude seemed to think about it. "Strange, yes. Eugene was odd. He had known the family in the old days, but not Paul, and he became stiff. Silent, for Eugene."

"Did Eugene mention Vel d'Hiv?"

"Not then, later at the shop. Vel d'Hiv was important to Paul Manet, eh? The large moment."

"But Manet didn't want to talk about it to Eugene?"

"No, he didn't."

"Was Eugene involved in Vel d'Hiv?

"No, at least not actively. He was there that night in Paris, and it had shaken him. Then, it shook many people once it was over. Not enough, though. It didn't shake enough good Frenchmen. Only Jews."

"Is Paul Manet a Jew?"

"No, not at all. That made him even more a hero, eh? His people were in no danger, yet he risked his life that night. So they say."

"He did, we've checked. No doubt of it."

"I'm sure he did. Heroes don't have to be any better than anyone else. Why not live on a moment of suffering? At least he acted then. One small clean path in a sea of guilt." Claude turned his dead eyes toward me. "Every country wants to see its people as patriot heroes. I grew up believing in France, my country; in the men and women who fought so bravely against the Germans. I despised those who had not fought, went out to fight for France myself. Only later, after I had seen what we did in Vietnam, in Algeria, did I find out. Only when I had already learned about countries and people did I learn."

In the silence his hands reached out for something, searching in the air, on the table near him. A drink, a glass in his hand, that was what he wanted. A companion. He found none.

"Claude?" Li said. "Don't talk about—"

He found a cigarette instead, smoked. "The truth is that only a pitiful few Frenchmen resisted. As many joined the Waffen SS as fought with the Free French, eh? That they did not tell the children of 1946. Paris went on eating at Maxim's, went on going to the races. Entertainers entertained—in Berlin. The great French Resistance was the work of a few British agents parachuted into France! Most of all, it was only the Communists who fought in large numbers, resisted the Nazis."

He laughed bitterly, an inner rage. "British agents! To organize Frenchmen to fight. No wonder Dienbienphu; sent to die for a ghost. Algeria—and Vel d'Hiv. If it were only France, I could fight, but it is everywhere, everyone. Vel d'Hiv."

"A Gestapo operation," I said. "Why—?"

His head came up, his eyes black. "Gestapo? All the Jews arrested that night were arrested by French gendarmes! Pétain agreed, Laval encouraged—they were only Jews, and non-French! The gendarmes were efficient, meticulous, even brutal. A few said no, a handful. The rest? Have you ever seen a policeman shrug, look away, while a child is dragged bewildered to death? Almost thirteen thousand were in Vel d'Hiv that night in 1942. Thirty adults came back after the war. Of four thousand children, none."

His black eyes were open sockets. "I was a child that night, Paris was not. Laval, Pétain were politicians like the corrupt in Hanoi, Saigon, Algiers. There are always monsters, they can be forgotten. The people cannot be forgotten. Paris. France. So few tried to stop it, fewer helped, still fewer cared as long as it wasn't them. The Dutch hid their Jews. The Danish King wore a yellow star himself and rode the streets of Copenhagen every day. The French rounded up the victims!"

I said, "Paul Manet was one who helped, fought. Yet there's something wrong about Manet. Something I think Eugene knew."

"He trades on his heroics," Claude Marais said, smoked. "Why not? If it was only France, only a few monsters, only that moment. But it isn't. I learned that in Indo-China, Algeria. All greed, lies, self-interest and power. No honor and no glory. Heroes are only fools sent to kill other fools."

"Claude," I said, "what did Eugene know about Paul Manet? Was there something back there in Paris?"

"Eugene did not know Paul Manet then, only some of his family. His mother, brother, grand—"

"Brother?" I said. "Younger or older?"

"Younger. A year or so."

"Was he in the Resistance too? The younger brother?"

"No, I don't think so."

"What happened to him, the younger brother?"

Claude shrugged. "He died, I think. In the chaos of 1945, the end of the Occupation. Eugene said something about that. To Paul Manet."

"The younger brother, *not* in the Resistance, died," I said, "and the older brother, active against the Germans, survived?"

"It happened in those days. It was all chaos, no one knew what would happen to whom. I think Paul Manet was captured, came back a year or so later. It is hard to know about those days. People vanished, reappeared, died, survived; no one knew how, or why, or what went on minute to minute."

"And papers were lost, destroyed," I said. "Faces changed with scars and suffering. If a man was captured by the Gestapo, did they announce it? Did they announce executions? Deaths?"

"No, a man simply disappeared. The Nazis themselves did not always know what happened to whom or where. Not at the end."

"Chaos," I said. "Stay here. Wait."

Claude Marais nodded. Li stood beside him.

23

Lieutenant Marx wasn't in his office. I talked to one of the other detectives.

"Tell Marx to contact Paris right now. Check out a younger brother of Paul Manet. Find out what happened to him, what Paul Manet did at the end of World War Two, where Paul was and where the younger brother was. Have them check records, photos, fingerprints if there are any. Find out if Paul Manet lived in Paris after the war, if he returned to his family and old friends. Especially check all records on the younger brother."

"You have something, Fortune?" the detective asked.

"I think so, a hunch. Tell Marx I'm going to try to find Charlie Burgos and Danielle Marais. A condemned building on Nineteenth Street, near the river. He'll know it."

The abandoned brownstone looked like any other building in the hot sun. No ghosts by day, only a shabby building with boards at the windows, people hurrying past on their important business, flowers on some of the weeds. No cars were in the alley.

Inside, the derelict building was dim and hot, and on the third floor there was no sound. In the room where I had been held, dark behind its blanketed windows, the mattresses were still there—but nothing else. Stripped, all the clothes and cheap possessions of the street boys gone. An empty room, as abandoned as the building itself.

Not quite.

Somewhere to the rear of the dark room there was a sound. A low sound—half like a whine, half a moan. I walked back, slowly and carefully.

She was kneeling on the bare floor—Danielle Marais. In tight blue jeans and an old shirt. She was crying, her head down, sitting back on her legs where she kneeled. She heard me behind her after a moment, looked back and up at me. Her heavy, petulant, juvenile face was anguished.

"He's dead. Someone killed him."

Charlie Burgos lay on his back, oddly flat like an animal with the meat sucked out. His sharp young face was etched in deep planes and furrows; somehow younger in the perpetual age of death. His wide eyes were shining as if he saw something very interesting on the ceiling of the barren room with its bare mattresses and blanket-covered windows. The handle of what looked like a hunting knife stuck up out of his chest like a cross, or the rifle of some soldier buried where he had fallen in an empty desert.

"I came to meet him," Danielle Marais said. "We were all going to meet. They ran, the others. Grabbed what they had, and ran. No one would stay with him. No one."

What else could they do, Charlie Burgos's brothers of the street? Powerless in a vast city, they could only run and hide and hope no one would think about them. Mice in a burning field, afraid of the flames and of the hawks that would soon come to hover over the blackened field looking for something to eat, preying on the exposed because they needed a victim.

"We were going away, it was going to be fine now," Danielle Marais said. "Fine, no more problems."

I knelt down over the body. There was a lot of blood. It had only just started to congeal, blacken. The knife handle was some kind of wrapped material—leather or plastic or a treated canvas that would give no fingerprints. A straight, colorless knife with only a small guard and a narrowish blade, but heavy. I felt Charlie Burgos. He was soft and limp, still vaguely warm. No more than two hours, even in the heat of the city, but probably not less than an hour.

"How long have you been here?" I asked Danielle.

She shook her head, back and forth. "I don't know. Maybe an hour, maybe more. I don't know. They just ran. They didn't even look at Charlie after they saw. Grabbed their dirty junk, and ran! His friends!"

"He's got no friends, he's dead," I said harshly. "That's the rules, Danielle. The law of the streets. He doesn't exist, and he never did now. That's the world you were going into, the world your father and mother wanted to save you from. You were going into it, and everyone in it wants only to escape into what you already have. You're lucky, a second chance."

She glared her hatred at me, but that would pass. To the young, poverty and clawing against an established world were exciting. But poverty is only pain, clawing only bleeds, and there is excitement and strength only when there is a choice.

"He's dead, Danielle," I said. "It's over. Do you know who killed him?"

"No," she said, stared down at Charlie Burgos dead in an empty building.

"But you know why, don't you? What was he doing, Danielle? What were you both doing?"

She shook her head. "I don't know! He never said—"

"Damn it, girl, you know, and whoever killed Charlie'll have to kill you too! Tell me! You saw something that night, right? Blackmail?"

"Yes, yes, yes!" she cried, rocked on her knees. "But I don't know who! Charlie didn't tell me who. He said it was better that way, safer. He was protecting me."

"Charlie Burgos? Nuts, he protected no one except himself. You weren't with him outside the pawn shop that night?"

"Not all the time," she said, tears in her eyes now as if the mention of that night made her remember all her times with Charlie Burgos. Maybe she had really loved him in her child's way—the worst, deepest way. "We'd gone to my father to borrow some money for an idea Charlie had. Dad wouldn't give us any. He was nice, he was always nice, but he said that Charlie was wrong for me, he wouldn't help Charlie to ruin me. We went out, we had nothing to do, you know, so we hung around. After the Chinaman came out, Charlie got restless waiting for Dad to come out. He sent—"

"Charlie was waiting for your father to come out? Why?"

She looked away. "I . . . I think he was going to rob the cash drawer. We knew there was money in it. I have a key."

"That sounds like Charlie," I agreed. "Why didn't he?"

"He . . . he saw someone. I . . . I think he did go into the shop, he had my key. I think that's why he sent me off."

"Sent you where?"

"He told me to come back here to the room to see if any of the boys were around and maybe had some money. He said he was thirsty, wanted a drink. But I think he sent me really because he didn't think I'd let him rob Dad's shop."

"What happened when you went back?"

"It took a while, you know? Over an hour. I waited here for one of the boys who was supposed to have money. Charlie got mad if he sent me for money and I didn't get any."

"I can believe that," I said. "An hour? Between eleven and twelve that night?"

She shook her head. "More like eleven-thirty to one A.M. He didn't send me right away after Jimmy Sung came out."

"When you did go back, what was Charlie doing?"

"Nothing—he wasn't there. I looked around, looked inside the shop. I . . . I found my Dad. He was in the chair—dead! I didn't know what to do. I thought—"

"That Charlie had killed him?"

She nodded, stared down at the dead boy. "So I came back here. Charlie was here. He said he hadn't killed Dad, but he knew who had! He said he'd seen who did it, seen him come out. We were going to be rich. He said we couldn't do anything for my father now, why not get rich? What did it matter if Dad's murderer was caught? It was better to be rich."

"He never told you who the killer was?"

"No," she said. "To protect me."

"Or because he thought maybe you wouldn't go along with the blackmail if you knew who the man was. Are you sure it was a man?"

"No, I'm not."

"Why were you around Paul Manet, Danielle?"

"Charlie sent me to him a couple of times. I took kind of messages. Mr. Manet was going to help Charlie get a job.

"A job? For Charlie?"

"That's what Charlie said."

"You never thought that Paul Manet could be the man Charlie was blackmailing? The killer he'd seen that night?"

"Mr. Manet? Why would he want to kill Dad? He was an old friend from Paris. He'd only just come to New York."

"Who really gave you that expensive dress, Danielle?'

"Charlie did. From the blackmail money."

"Then why would Paul Manet say he bought it?"

"I . . . I don't know. I was glad he did. I mean, I knew I'd made a mistake when I told you Charlie had bought it. You'd guess Charlie was up to something if he had that kind of money, so I was glad when Mr. Manet said he bought it for me, but I don't know why he said it."

I said, "I do."

24

Paul Manet was back in his work clothes—another expensive, pale blue suit with a hint of military epaulets and a slim, belted waist. I pushed him into the plush, sunken living room of Jules Rosenthal, a man only too glad to lend his palace to a hero of France.

"What are you doing!"

That was all, his whole protest. A man four inches taller, thirty pounds heavier, and with two arms. It was amazing he had gotten away with it so long. Smart and very careful. He backed away from me, looked toward Danielle, his fine face suddenly pale. It was Danielle being there that turned him pale, haggard.

"Charlie Burgos was blackmailing you," I said. "That's why you covered that slip Danielle made about the dress. You didn't want me to know that Charlie Burgos had sudden money."

"That is a lie."

Part of the success of his masquerade was habit. The habit of a lot of years. Pale, he still acted out his role—the officer and gentleman defying the common herd.

"You met Eugene Marais that night. Between midnight and one A.M. Charlie Burgos saw you. He saw you go into the shop, and he saw you come out—after you killed Eugene Marais."

"No!" His voice was strangled now.

"Yes," I said, "and I know why. I know who you really are."

I waited. He said nothing. Shook his head.

"The police are checking with Paris," I said. "They're asking what happened to Paul Manet in the war-end chaos of 1945, and what happened to Paul Manet's younger brother. Not much younger; a year or

two. What's you real name, Manet? What was the name you abandoned when you took over the identity and history of your brother
Paul? The real name that Eugene Marais knew?"

Whatever his real first name was, he shook his head in the gaudy
living room of the luxury apartment. The kind of place he had become
accustomed to living in, being given by grateful Frenchmen, in all the
years since World War II.

"Eugene Marais knew you. Maybe not at once. In the Balzac
Union he watched you, puzzled at first. He wasn't sure what seemed
wrong to him, was he? But you knew. Since the war you had avoided
anyone who knew Paul well, and explained any facial differences by
Nazi torture. I'll bet you told a beautiful story. People like to know a
hero, had no reason to doubt you. Eugene Marais hadn't known Paul,
but he had known *you*—the younger brother! You'd never thought of
that. Who would remember the unknown brother of a national hero?
An old friend of the family with a long memory, that's who, and you
saw at once that Eugene was puzzled. You've probably got a sixth
sense by now, and you saw that Eugene had seen something.

"So you avoided him at the Balzac Union. Only, by accident, you
met Eugene outside the Union. Talking to you up close, Eugene saw
it. He realized that you weren't Paul Manet, you were the younger
brother. Eugene Marais wasn't a man who acted rashly. He thought
about it, talked around the subject to Claude, considered it all. He
even talked to you about it, and sensed you'd like to see him silenced.
'Even a man who has done nothing, there will be reasons for some to
want him gone, nonexistent.' He said that.

"You were in danger of losing all you had, because it's all based
on Paul Manet's reputation. So you went to the pawn shop, but too
many people were there at five. You made a date to meet Eugene that
night—and you kept the date. You went to the shop, killed him, faked
the robbery, and left. But Charlie Burgos saw you. You had to pay him
to keep silent. Only paying a man isn't as safe or sure as killing him. Not
with me and the cops still looking. So today you killed Charlie Burgos."

Manet flinched at each word as if I were slapping him on the face. He stood rigid, like a spy being interrogated. But when I said that he had killed Charlie Burgos, he moved.

"Charlie Burgos? Dead? No."

"Stabbed in his rooms not two hours ago. I'd say he was killed right after Li Marais and I left here. After you saw that I was still looking for Eugene Marais's killer."

"Two hours?" Manet said, began to smile. "Two hours? Then . . . then I couldn't have killed him! No. I could not have killed Burgos." He laughed. "Just before you came here this morning I had been on the telephone to Paris for over an hour. You can verify that, I can name who I talked to. When you and that Oriental woman arrived, I had just hung up. After you left me earlier, four businessmen came here to discuss imports. All known men, above suspicion. They came immediately after you left, went away just before you and Danielle arrived this time. I'm surprised you did not meet them both times. I have not been from this apartment all day. There is no way I could have murdered Charlie Burgos!"

It had the sound of truth. It would be too easy to disprove if it wasn't true. His smile had the truth in it too. The smile of a man who knew he was clear, safe. Someone else had killed Charlie Burgos. Maybe one of Charlie's own street kids over the blackmail money.

"Maybe you didn't kill Burgos," I said, "but you did kill Eugene Marais."

"No!" Manet was almost eager. "Someone who killed Burgos, also killed Eugene Marais. Don't you see? Charlie Burgos must have been blackmailing someone else besides me! The murderer of Eugene Marais."

He was excited, almost happy. Sure that he had just made me see his innocence. I saw, heard, something else.

"So," I said, "you admit that Charlie Burgos *was* blackmailing you. Why? For spitting on the sidewalk?"

"I . . . I—" He licked at his lips.

I said, "The police will be here soon. They'll have found Charlie Burgos, they'll know I'm here. They'll have the information from Paris. They'll know what Eugene Marais knew, and why you killed him."

For a moment more, he stood tall. Then he sat down. On a hard, narrow chair. It was too small for his size. He didn't seem to notice that. He noticed his hands instead. Looked at them, turned them over, as if wondering who they really belonged to.

"Burgos was blackmailing me," he said finally. "If you have asked about Paul Manet's younger brother in Paris, it will all come out." He looked up at me. "Yes, I was at the pawn shop that night. Yes, Burgos saw me. Yes, I have been posing as my brother for twenty-six years. I am Fernand Manet, the younger brother of Paul, and Eugene Marais did know me."

He clasped his hands between his legs until the knuckles cracked. He touched the soft cloth of his pale blue trousers, the perfect crease. He touched the cloth almost lovingly.

"If you had been there in Paris at the end of the war, you would understand," Manet said. "The confusion, the deaths, the disappearances, the miraculous escapes. In a way it was so simple to become Paul."

He looked at me. "I was only a year younger than Paul. I could have joined the Resistance. My mother said that one son was enough for France. I let her think that I wanted to join the Resistance like Paul, but that she had convinced me not to for her sake. But that was a lie. I didn't want to join, I was never brave. I could never have faced the Gestapo."

"Not many could," I said. "Not many did."

He ignored me. "The war was almost over. The heroes would get the respect, the cheers, the rewards. We had heard from Paul's comrades that he had been arrested in early 1945. He had been sent to Germany. Perhaps to Dachau or Belsen. No one survived Dachau or Belsen."

His eyes flinched again, remembered those days. "The last week of the war, the Germans rounded up all the men left on my street. They shot my mother. My grandfather was already dead. We had no father. They took me with hundreds of others to a place outside Paris.

There were only a few Germans. The Americans were very close. The German officers saw their men melting away, trying to escape into Germany, deserting. One day the officers told their men to shoot us all, en masse. But they couldn't shoot us all. There were hundreds and more of us, too few of them, many of us escaped. I was one of the lucky. I hid for days in an old cistern. At last the Americans came. Alone, my papers lost the day they shot us, I walked to Paris."

The wild confusion of Paris liberated was in Manet's face. "Some Maquis patrol stopped me far from my section. They were suspicious of a man without papers, but one of them stared at me, asked my name. I told them—Manet. The one man became excited. I realized that he thought I was Paul! He told the others. They were pleased, eager. All at once I was Paul, the returned hero.

"That one Maquis knew Paul by sight, by reputation, by background. He didn't *really* know Paul. I had a beard, was in rags and filthy, and Paul and I did look much alike—the same height, hair, eyes, build. They questioned me, of course, but I knew Paul's life as well as my own. Convinced, they passed me safely on to Free French troops who knew Paul only by his exploits."

His eyes were bright. "I was a hero. Admired. I liked it. At first I planned to disappear fairly soon, become myself again. But then I found out that Paul's whole cell had been arrested with him. No one seemed to doubt me. There were many who had known Paul a little who obviously believed I was him. Our whole family was dead. Paul was certainly dead. Why not *be* Paul? If he did come back some day, I would tell him the truth.

"So I became Paul. I was careful. I never went back to our old street. I avoided anyone who might have known Paul more than to say hello to. Finally, my real papers were found near some of those shot the day I escaped. I made my final step—I identified an unclaimed body as myself: Fernand Manet. So Fernand Manet, a nobody, was dead. Paul Manet, a hero, was alive."

He stopped. I gave him a cigarette. He lit it. "Paul never came back. There are no records of what happened to him. I was a hero;

admired and honored. Jewish companies who knew what Paul had done at Vel d'Hiv gave me good jobs. At last I hit on my present work—the hero representative abroad. No one would know Paul abroad. I do my work well. I earn my rewards."

There was a faint hint of the fake aristocratic pride he had learned so well over the years. Perhaps his work was based on a lie, but he had done it well. He had his pride.

"But Eugene Marais did know you," I said. "Not Paul Manet. He knew Fernand Manet."

Manet nodded. "Yes, he guessed. We talked. I denied it, but there are small scars, a birthmark on my neck, some mannerisms I barely knew I have but Eugene remembered. He wasn't absolutely sure, and I denied it, but what if he decided to raise the question back in France? A doubt would be enough to ruin me. I tried to pay him. He refused. I sensed that he was trying to decide what he should do. So I made the appointment to meet him that night. I took a gun. I might have killed him, I don't know. But I didn't kill him. When I got to the shop, the door was unlocked. He was in the back room in the chair, dead!"

"What time was it when you say you got there?"

"About midnight. A little after. I can't be sure."

"What did you do?"

"I . . . I panicked." He licked at his lips again. "I mean, I might have gone to kill him. I had a gun. I was there, he was dead, and I had a gun! Maybe it was guilt in me, but I was in that shop alone with a gun and a dead man and I panicked. What if I had been seen? What if someone knew I had reason to want Marais dead? I decided to make it look like robbery. I grabbed objects at random, packed them in a suitcase. I left. I took the suitcase to that Salvation Army mission. Then I came home here."

Now his ravaged eyes looked up. "Ten minutes after I got home, that Charlie Burgos called me. He had seen me. He had found Eugene dead in the shop. He knew who I was from Danielle earlier. I paid him a thousand dollars, three more thousand since. What else could I do? I would be accused of murder!"

I let him sit there in silence, sweating under that beautiful suit. Danielle was sitting on the raised step in the entrance archway to the sunken living room. Jules Rosenthal's room, a man grateful for a hero's help to the Jews. Down the corridor outside, the elevator stopped at the floor.

"You know," I said, "I don't think Eugene Marais would ever have exposed you. Not in the end. A kind man."

"How could I know?" Manet said. "But I didn't kill him."

"Sure," I said.

I heard them in the corridor just before the doorbell rang. Danielle opened the door. Lieutenant Marx and his two men came in. I waited for them standing over Manet.

"I figured you'd be here," Marx said. "We found Charlie Burgos. What about Manet?"

"He didn't kill Charlie, but he's a fake, and I figure he killed Eugene Marais."

I told him all Manet had told me. Marx listened while his men inspected the lush apartment, whistling with awe over it. When I finished, Marx looked down at Manet.

"He was dead when you got to the shop around midnight, maybe twelve-fifteen? You faked the robbery?"

Manet nodded. "I panicked, but he was dead."

"How long had he been dead, would you say?"

"Not very long. He was . . . warm."

"Did you see a package in the back room? Maybe took it?"

"I saw no package. There wasn't a package, I'm sure."

Marx nodded slowly. I swore.

"Damn it, he's lying," I said. "He has to be. He had the motive, he was there, he was paying Charlie Burgos. He killed Eugene Marais."

"No!" Manet cried, stood up, swayed.

"No," Lieutenant Marx said. "I believe him. We picked up the killer of Charlie Burgos ten minutes ago, Dan, and I figure the same killer for Eugene Marais."

25

I said, "Who?"

"We identified the knife, Dan," Marx said. "You never pulled it out, right? Touch nothing?"

"Damn it, Marx, who?"

"Claude Marais," Marx said. "We knew he killed his brother. But with you, Kandinsky and the French making noise, and no direct evidence against him, we decided to let him go, give him rope, and watch him. We don't apologize."

"Claude?" I said. "No, I don't believe it."

"When we let him go, we put a tail on him, of course. He slipped our tail right after leaving jail. It looked like it could have been an accident—our man just missed a lucky subway train. I chewed our man out, he made a mistake. We never expected Claude would kill anyone else. We can't cover every possibility. It was a risk."

"Why did Claude kill Charlie Burgos?" I said.

"The way I see it," Marx said, "Charlie Burgos saw *two* men that night at the shop. He saw Claude Marais go in *first*. He saw Claude come out about midnight carrying the package of diamonds. Minutes later, before Charlie had time to look in the shop, Manet showed up and went inside. After Manet came out with the suitcase, Charlie went inside the shop and found Eugene Marais dead. That gave Charlie *two* pigeons."

"How did Charlie know which one killed Marais?"

"I don't figure he did, not for sure. In fact, that can explain a lot of what else happened later," Marx said. "Manet paid him, so Charlie must have figured Manet was the killer. I think Claude Marais held out, so Charlie figured Claude was innocent. Of the murder, anyway. But

Claude had been there, had taken that package. Charlie didn't know what was in the package, but he knew Claude was lying about being there at all. So Charlie phoned in the tip on the package to put pressure on Claude to pay him to keep quiet.

"Charlie had a beautiful double play. He figured Claude wasn't a killer, we'd let Claude go, but Charlie would have proved to Claude it was better to pay him than have him talk. If we didn't let Claude go, that would give Charlie an even tighter hold on Manet. With Claude accused, even convicted, Manet would be really safe—as long as Charlie said nothing. Only Charlie Burgos made one big mistake—he had the wrong killer. Claude killed Eugene, and Charlie Burgos was the one man who could prove it. So exit Charlie."

It was good. Very good. Logical.

"How do you prove all that? Charlie Burgos is dead."

"We don't prove it, Dan, unless Claude Marais wants to tell us. Maybe he will now, we've got him cold for Charlie Burgos. If he won't talk, we'll convict him for Charlie only. But he killed Eugene too. It's his only possible motive for killing Charlie Burgos."

"What was on that knife that proves Claude killed Burgos?"

"French army stuff all over the blade—Thirteenth Half Brigade," Marx said. "And Claude's initials etched near the hilt. We already knew that Claude had a knife—a souvenir. It was in his bag the night we first arrested him, and it's not there now. The sheath was in that condemned house, too."

"He left a knife marked like that? Left it in the body? You can't believe it, Marx!"

Marx shrugged. "Panic. We've both seen it too often, Dan. Charlie hadn't been dead long when Danielle and those street kids found him. Claude heard them coming, panicked, and ran."

"It takes seconds to pull out a knife. A trained man like Claude wouldn't let go of a knife when he struck. He'd have stabbed, pulled it back out ready to hit again."

Marx's voice was quiet. "It was stuck hard in a rib, Dan. Took two of us to get it out. I can see him trying to pull it out when he heard someone coming. It wouldn't come out. So then he had to leave it, run before he was discovered."

"No," I said. "He's too cool, too trained."

"Maybe," Marx said, "but he's a strange one. Mixed up. Maybe he wanted to be caught. We'll ask the psychiatrists. He wanted Burgos dead, didn't care if he was caught. To hell with the world. He's got to be half crazy, Dan."

"You said that about Jimmy Sung."

"Sometimes we're wrong, sometimes we're right. Maybe Claude just doesn't care what happens to him anymore, has a reason not to care. You might even know the reason, Dan."

As I've said before, the police don't miss much. Did I know a reason for Claude Marais not to give a damn anymore? Yes, I did, didn't I? Li Marais. If he knew about us? Maybe if I'd been Claude, I'd want to be locked up too—after I'd killed a rat that had been chewing at me.

"What does Claude have to say this time?"

"Denies it," Marx said. "But he admits the knife is his, and after he lost our man following him, he says he just went walking around. He even admits that as far as he knows, no one could have taken his knife."

I had nothing more to say. What could I say? If it was a frame-up, I had no ideas about who. As far as Lieutenant Marx was concerned, he had his man this time. He took Paul (Fernand) Manet when he left. There was a technical charge of robbery, and a real charge of failing to report a murder. Manet's masquerade was over.

It was late afternoon now, the sun bright on the hot city. But in her hotel suite, Li Marais sat in the dark behind the drawn shades. I sat facing her.

"Are you all right?" I said.

"Yes."

Her smooth face was like stone again. I moved in my chair. Her eyes flickered toward me.

"No, not now," she said. "Not this time."

"I didn't come for that," I said.

She nodded faintly. "This time they will not let him go." A light breeze stirred the drawn shades, but not her face. Motionless in the shadows, she could have been a statue in some ancient temple. "Perhaps this time he does not want them to let him go."

"Did he do it, Li? Both murders?"

The traffic down in the street was heavy and distant. In the hotel room the city seemed far away. When she spoke, her lips hardly moved, like a graven image with a tape recorder inside.

"When they came he did not protest. He could not say what he had done since he was released this morning. He had taken money from our bank, he will not say why. When could someone have taken his knife? Since he was first arrested, I left this suite very little. I am sure no one has been here except you. He is accomplished with his knife."

"An expert," I said. "He shouldn't have hit a rib."

"He has not used his knife in many years."

"Li?" I said, "could he have killed Eugene? We know the exact time now: between eleven P.M. when Jimmy Sung left, and about twelve-twenty when Charlie Burgos must have found him dead. You said that Claude was here with you the night Eugene was killed—from before ten P.M., until he left about three A.M. Were you lying? The police have to think you lied. If you were telling the truth, we'll go on fighting."

"I did not lie. I did not tell the truth."

"Not both, no. Li, I've got to know—"

She stopped me without moving. A silent force that filled the dim room. "To me he was here all the time that night. He was here when I went to sleep at eleven-thirty. He was here when I woke up at three A.M. to find him dressed and ready to go out. I did not question that he had not left. But we are not husband and wife, you understand? I was in bed in the bedroom. Claude was here in the living room on the couch. The door between us was closed. I was asleep."

I understood the police now. Had Claude left this suite for very long, Li might have awakened and missed him. But he could easily have slipped out briefly. Ten minutes to the pawn shop at a fast walk, ten minutes back. I had been gone from the lobby by eleven-thirty that night. Claude could have gone to the pawn shop, killed Eugene, and been back in his suite by twelve-thirty or so. Easily, and Li not waking up at all.

"Is he sick, Li?"

"Yes. Of many things."

"Then you think he did it? Killed them?"

"No, he did not kill them."

"How do we prove that? How do we even know?"

"You cannot prove it."

"Can you know, Li? Can you really be sure?"

"I am sure," she said. She was the way I had first seen her that day in the pawn shop with Claude and Eugene—small, hardly there at all, almost translucent. "I remember the knife the evening we were here when he was first arrested. It was in his suitcase as it always was. I saw it. I do not remember seeing it again. I remember the hat badge that was found in the register. I remember it on his bureau among loose cuff links and old keys. I remember I saw it."

"On what bureau did you see it? When?"

"In the bedroom. Earlier that same day it was found in the register. His hat badge."

"That's bad for him, Li."

"Yes, bad."

"What can we do, Li? They have the circumstances for Eugene, the knife for Charlie Burgos. Motive for both, and one killing proves the other."

"You can do nothing, Dan."

I heard something in her voice? What? Her voice that dismissed all effort to help Claude. Why?

"If Claude didn't kill them, Li, he's being framed. Who by, and why?"

For a moment she didn't answer me. Then, "His uniform is in our closet. The image of France. I do not know why he kept it. For me, perhaps. I married him in it. Soon after we came here, Viviane asked him to wear it to the shop for Danielle. Once. With its medals, its boots, its beret, its *élan*. I remember how all the people stared. A French soldier."

I waited, but that was all. I sensed that she was telling me something. What? I sensed that she was going to do something. What?

"Li? What are you going to do?"

"Wait," she said. "I am going to wait."

"Li," I said, "I'll go on trying. I'll work on."

"Yes," she said.

The bedroom door was open, the bed ready. I had lost one woman this summer. We were both alone now, but somehow I knew that the bed was not ready for me this time.

"You want me to go, Li?"

She didn't answer, fading away from me in the hot room, going from translucent to transparent, vanishing. Into another world, an alien world, where I couldn't follow. Into an alien world where she would do something, but where I did not know what it would be. I sensed her slipping away, and her purpose, and there was nothing I could do except try to prove that Claude Marais was innocent. If he was.

26

I sensed that if I was going to help Li, I had to do it fast. Prove Claude innocent or guilty once and for all, and fast.

I looked for witnesses. All that evening and night. For anyone who might have seen someone else at the pawn shop on the night Eugene Marais died. For anyone who had seen someone else at the condemned house of Charlie Burgos this morning. I knocked on doors, buttonholed shopkeepers, and all I found was a woman who had seen a man at the condemned building around noon today. A shabby man with one arm. Me.

I couldn't see Claude Marais until morning. I went home. My five rooms were hot and lonely. The extra loneliness of knowing that someone who had been there often would not be there again.

I sat with a beer and thought about what to do next. I could knock on more doors, ask more questions, go around it all again to see if I could have missed something.

I drank beer, and watched television, and went to bed.

Captain Olsen, Gazzo's fill-in, was with Lieutenant Marx in his office the next morning. I could talk to Claude Marais at noon, not that it would do me any good.

"Even that lawyer Kandinsky isn't saying much this time," Captain Olsen said. "Marais'll talk soon. They always talk in the end."

"No confession yet?" I said. "That's funny, if he wants to be locked up so badly. Leaving that knife and all."

"You're saying it's a frame-up," Marx said. A statement, not a question. "Marais isn't saying it's a frame-up. You'd think he'd be shouting it if he thought it was."

"Unless," Captain Olsen said, "you think he's protecting someone. Maybe you think that, Fortune? Who could it be?"

I leaned on the wall of the office, but I was alert. Were they playing with me? Or did they know something?

"Who would he protect?" I said.

"Yeh, who?" Marx said. "We've booked Manet for not reporting. We'll drop the robbery, make it obstructing in a murder. He's going to know what it's really like being a prisoner after all. The report came from Paris, it fits. They don't much like it over there. The French won't defend Manet this time."

"We like our people all to be heroes," I said.

Captain Olsen said, "The wife, maybe? Or the sister-in-law, Viviane Marais? Or the girl, Danielle? Claude might try to protect them. The trouble is, we can't think of any motives for them to have killed Eugene Marais at all."

"That knife," I said, "it bothers you. So stupid."

"We've got to believe it, though," Captain Olsen said.

"A half-crazy killer," Marx said. "War experiences."

"You'll convince a jury," I said. "If it's a frame-up, it's a very good one."

"We don't want to convince a jury," Marx said.

Captain Olsen was going to add something, maybe about who they did want to convince, but I never knew what it was. The telephone rang. Marx listened. First idly, then with a frown, then alert. He said, "Yes," and hung up. He stood up.

"The wife," Marx said. "That was some priest. Noyoda, or something like that. He says the wife, Li Marais, is down on the steps of his temple. She's going to burn herself on his temple steps!"

I saw her, Li, from three blocks away. Lieutenant Marx cursed at his driver to go faster through the narrow Chinatown street that was clotted with traffic. The driver swore back, inched along the street blocked by the cars, pushcarts, and people of Chinatown.

I watched only Li Marais in the distance. Alone on the three steps of the Buddhist temple.

I could see her clear. The block of the temple as empty as the next block was crowded. A deserted street in front of the temple in the distance, the people gathered a hundred feet away on either side—from fear or respect I never would know.

She was a tiny, distant figure all in yellow. Saffron yellow. A kneeling doll in a saffron robe, her head down in prayer or meditation or both. What did it matter?

We were still two blocks away, blocked in the traffic and crowd, when I saw her tiny yellow figure move.

"Li!" I shouted. A shout into the wind.

The flames exploded around her. In the distance on those temple steps she was engulfed in flames in a second.

"Gasoline," the driver said. "Christ."

"God damn!" Marx said.

We got out and ran. The last two blocks. We ran, knocking people away, but even the last small flames were fading by the time we reached her.

Lieutenant Marx went to her. She was dead. Only the black, charred shape of what had been one small woman. A human being.

Marx went to her, I couldn't. For her last words to me? What was Dan Fortune to her? There were no words anyway. There wouldn't have been even if a spark of life had still been in her. Li Marais had said all that she had to say.

Marx cursed his driver, sent him for the ambulance. It couldn't help, but Marx had to do something. She had done her work too well. Perhaps she had cheated just a little. She had been away from the Orient and Buddha a long time. A small poison pill to make it quicker? I hoped she had.

The priest, Noyoda, stood over her with us. Some of the people were down on their knees now. Marx swore at Noyoda. The Lieutenant was white. To our Western minds, it's a horrible form of suicide.

"You let her!" Marx shouted at Noyoda. "That's a crime, you hear, mister? Why didn't you stop her?"

"I could not stop her," Noyoda said.

He meant, I knew, that by his beliefs he could not stop a believer who wanted to immolate herself, perform her special devotion, improve her life and her eternity. But Noyoda was an American, too. He knew the law.

"She poured the gasoline on herself before I discovered her on the steps," Noyoda said. "She had a cigarette lighter in her hand. She said she would light the flame as soon as anyone came near her. I did all I could, and I called you."

He was right, of course. The empty gasoline can lay some yards to the right. The cigarette lighter lay blackened near Li Marais. Marx could do nothing to Noyoda.

"So it was her after all," Marx said as the ambulance began to wail up in the distance. "She killed them after all."

"No," I said. "She was with me when Charlie was killed."

"Killed?" Noyoda said.

I explained the murders to the priest.

"Buddhists do not commit suicide to escape their own guilt or problems," Noyoda said. "Almost never."

Marx nodded. "She couldn't have killed Charlie Burgos, I guess that's sure. Distraught, Dan? She knew Claude Marais killed them both, and couldn't go on alone?"

"I don't think so, Marx," I said. "For a Buddhist, suicide, especially this way, is a positive act."

"Positive? How in hell is it positive?" Marx swore.

Noyoda said, "You have arrested her husband for these murders? Is there any doubt that he is guilty?"

"None," Marx snapped. "If she figured to fool us—"

"She thought there was doubt," I said. "So do I."

Noyoda looked down at Li Marais's charred body. The ambulance had arrived, the doctor just looking at the body too. Noyoda reached into his pocket.

"Then I think I can say why she did this," the priest said.

He handed Marx a piece of letter stationery. It was Hotel Stratford stationery. I read the note on it with Marx: *My flame will light the truth.*

"I think," Noyoda said, sadly now, "she has done this to make you seek the truth, Lieutenant. Her death was to make you know her husband is innocent, make you find the truth."

"Crazy," Marx said, watched the ambulance men put the dead Li into their basket. "What a lousy, useless thing to do. For nothing."

"Useless?" Noyoda stared at Marx. "You are a fool, Lieutenant. You are impertinent and insulting!"

The priest walked into his temple. I could hear the chanting going on inside the temple already. They would chant for a long time. Marx stared after the angry priest.

"What the hell is that all about?"

"Religion," I said. "To Buddhists, a man is composed of two elements, Lieutenant. The manas, the organ of understanding; and the karma, the entirety of the acts accomplished in the course of his life. When a man dies, the manas, the understanding organ, pass into another body—higher or lower in quality according to the quality of the karma, what he has done on earth. If the karma has been exceptional, then there is no reincarnation, the man has attained nirvana. So for a devout Buddhist, suicide for some noble purpose—like freeing an innocent man—is a way to improve his karma, make himself much better, and maybe even achieve nirvana."

"You think Li Marais believed all that?"

I watched the ambulance drive away. "I'm not sure. To any good Buddhist, though, it would be self-evident. It would be understood right away."

"Damn it," Marx said, "I'm an American cop, not a Buddhist. You think she really thought she could influence the police this way? Make us see we had to be wrong? It's crazy, Dan."

"A Buddhist believes that by suicide he creates problems for the person responsible for forcing him to do it, one way or another," I said slowly. "It's an infallible way of making someone know they are wrong. To a Buddhist, no one could be indifferent to that. The truth must come out."

"You think it was all for us? The police?"

"Maybe," I said, "but she'd been in the western world a long time. She knew about American police, she knew it would mean nothing to you. She was distraught, maybe, but she wasn't a fool."

"Then what the hell was she doing?" Marx said. "Do you know, Dan?"

"I think so," I said.

27

I said I thought I knew what Li Marais expected her death to do. That was all I said.

Marx swore at me. But if I'd said any more, Marx would have ruined it. Ruined her death, what she had done it for.

"I'll explain when I'm sure," I said to Marx.

If I was right, what she had done it for would take a little time. The major reason she had ended her life.

I didn't kid myself that another reason hadn't been guilt, maybe shame. For what she and I had done. She had betrayed Claude Marais, he was in real trouble, and she had to help him. Help and atone. I had to face it. I had bad nights while I waited for what I was sure she had expected to happen next.

I waited three days.

My flame will light the truth. Had she made a mistake? Her flaming death a tragic miscalculation? I had the sick feeling that it had been. A straw she had grasped at, almost hopeless, and maybe she hadn't really cared if her death was useless.

But I cared.

After three days, I had to act.

The woman, Marie Schmidt, opened the door of the tenement apartment. Her ugly face had lost its snap and vigor.

"He's in the back room. It's not locked," she said. "Three days in and out of back there. No sleep. Like a crazy tiger in a cage. I can't take no more. He scares me now."

I went through the spartan living room. I had my old gun in my pocket. The outer door closed behind me. Marie Schmidt hurried away down the stairs Jimmy Sung kept so clean.

I opened the door of the empty back room. It wasn't empty now.

Flags hung on the walls—Chinese Communist flags, Viet Cong flags, flags I didn't even recognize. Giant photos of Mao Tse-tung. Modern Chinese rifles, and ancient muskets. Swords and curved knives. Portraits of Confucius and Genghis Khan. Mongol helmets with horsehair hanging. A map of China. A painted Buddha. An ancient map of the Mongol Empire stretching far into Europe. A photo of the Chinese H-bomb test. Parades of Chinese youths. Headlines from New York newspapers during the Korean War—all of Chinese victories.

The room a hymn to China. Powerful—and yet confused. Not all China, and irrational. Madame Chiang was there, and photos of the rich Soongs. Ho Chi Minh, and some Chinese emperors. The Burmese U Thant, Japanese soldiers in a *banzai* celebration of some victory over America. A samurai sword beside an ancient Mongol lance. A twisted celebration of Asian glory that filled the room, hidden perhaps for years in an open trunk that stood in a corner of the room.

Among it all, Jimmy Sung kneeled before the small jade Buddha. Incense burned, and a half-empty quart of vodka was on the floor beside Jimmy Sung. He drank as I watched, shivered. He wore the padded blue uniform of a Chinese soldier, and another samurai sword was near his hand.

"How long have you had all this, Jimmy?" I said.

He turned to look at me. His face was like the hundred-year-old woman in Shangri-La who had never aged, and who then aged the whole hundred years in a single moment. Wasted, ravaged.

"Long time," Jimmy said, slurred. "Long damn time."

He was drunk. But how drunk? On that plateau where he functioned, or over the edge? A manic shine to his dark eyes.

"Where did it all come from, Jimmy?" I said.

"All over. Junk shops, Chinamen shops, sailors," he said, nodded as if agreeing with himself. A sudden cunning grin. "I get from dumb soldiers back from Korea, Vietnam. I make them think we all friends, buy the souvenirs, and inside I'm cheerin' for China, Viet Cong—the 'gooks'!"

"You've lived in America all your life, Jimmy."

He spat on the floor. "Lousy Chinaman! Chink!" He hunched where he still kneeled. "We are great people, great culture. In time of the Khans we ruled the world. Great teachers, wise men."

"You should have gone back, Jimmy."

"No way. I dream, but no way. Only here, spit on."

I watched him drink the vodka. He dreamed of China, but somewhere inside him he knew it was an insane dream. America was the only real world he knew. China would be an alien place. In his small, rational core, he didn't really want to go back. But alone in an America that ignored him, he had to dream. He had to believe in his hidden dream, and now he was tortured, confused. Three days tortured in this dream room because Li Marais had immolated herself to reach him.

"*My flame will light the truth*," I said. "Li Marais knew her suicide wouldn't touch the police. That wasn't why she did it. She did it to make you tell the truth. A Buddhist way to force another Buddhist. She knew that you killed Eugene Marais and Charlie Burgos."

Jimmy Sung thrashed at an invisible stake, tried to deny it even to himself. "Crazy woman! Liar."

"She told me the day they arrested Claude Marais the second time," I said, "but I didn't understand her. She didn't want me to understand. Not then. She said she had seen the hat badge on Claude's bureau, had seen the knife in his suitcase. She meant that she remembered that she had seen both the badge and the knife in the suite on that day the police first arrested Claude. They had been there in sight. The hat badge had not been in the register with the package. That evening when you were so brave against Gerd Exner."

"Chinese are brave," Jimmy Sung said. "Strong. Yeh."

"You had put that package of diamonds into the register, you went to the suite to talk to Li Marais a lot. After the detective found the package, while we all looked at the diamonds, you just walked into the bedroom, got the hat badge, and said you'd found it in the register. Who thought of doubting that you had? How could Claude Marais have denied it, even if he had remembered where he'd last seen his badge? You took the knife then, too. No one was going to search you. No reason to. You'd been cleared of any robbery, and what other motive did you have to kill Eugene Marais or anyone?"

"My friend, Mr. Marais," Jimmy Sung said, nodded to himself.

"But when Claude was arrested for killing Charlie Burgos, Li Marais began to think. She was sure Claude was innocent. She knew Manet couldn't have killed Burgos. So who was framing Claude? Why? That was when she realized it had to be you, Jimmy. She realized what the motive was, and killed herself to make you tell the truth and save Claude."

I talked, but in that hot room I felt unreal. A room that was a museum to an illusion. An illusion that battled with the real world where Jimmy Sung had lived his bleak life. A battle that had gone on inside him now for three days. A struggle, started by Li Marais in her death, that moved Jimmy Sung between the real world of America, and the illusion world of China.

"Li knew," I said, "because she realized that, in part, you had killed for *her*. It wasn't Eugene Marais you wanted dead, it was Claude Marais. Eugene was an accident. It was Claude you wanted to kill."

"That Claude!" Jimmy Sung drank, drank again. "Medals. French hero. Steal women, steal everything. Steal countries, murder babies, kill my people, get medals."

I had heard almost the same words before, but I hadn't been listening. I had been thinking of other things that day in the bar when Jimmy Sung had been released from jail.

"Claude Marais," I said. "The enemy. In the pawn shop in full uniform. The enemy who stole a child bride."

Jimmy Sung shook where he kneeled in the room of his secret world. More than half drunk. Scared in one world, proud in the other. Hate for Claude Marais and his uniform, and more than a little in love with Li Marais. A dream of Li Marais, too. That had to be part of it. An illusion of China, and of a woman, and of Buddha. Of a religion that demanded the truth now.

"All lies," Jimmy said. "That Claude. Steal a kid."

He was balanced on a hair. Half of him lived in America, and a man did not convict himself of murder because a woman burned herself to death in a yellow robe. But the other half lived in the illusion of China, of Buddha, where he was better, stronger and prouder than the white men who looked at him but never saw him. Balanced on the edge between.

"Lies," he said. "No one knows. Who will know?"

He talked to himself, his shadow inside. Ripped up between his empty real world of America, and his glorious illusion world of China. Aware of the danger to him in the real world if he acted by his illusion, but aware, deep inside him, that if he did not act according to his illusion he would lose his dream forever. If he denied the reality of China and Buddha now, he could never believe in it again. A drunken zero with no name in a world that ignored him. All he needed was a push.

"I'll know, Jimmy," I said. "And Claude Marais will know. Claude Marais will know the truth about you. No Buddhist, no believer, no man of China. Claude will know, and Li."

"That Claude!" Jimmy glared his hate.

"A man of China would have to tell the truth," I said.

Silent, he kneeled there. In his padded blue uniform, under his flags, and maps, and guns. He shook, but a little less now. He stared at the small, jade Buddha in front of him.

"Truth?" he said. "I have to tell the truth. To Buddha."

"Yes," I said. "The only way. For Li Marais."

"Yes," he said.

He said it, and he shook, and after a time I saw that he was crying. A crying jag. Self pity? Or maybe he cried for something else.

I found his telephone, called Lieutenant Marx.

No matter how it begins, or why, it ends in a windowless room with the pencil scrape of a stenographer. Marx nodded in the interrogation room. Jimmy began to talk:

"That Claude! Colonial bastard. I know about the French. I am Chinese, a great people. In the time of the Khans, we rule the world. We do it again. We finish all you white men never see no one. Real free, you know? For everyone. Not laugh at no one. We don't put someone in a crazy house just 'cause he don't talk English, is scared, got no friends. We don't tell lies, spit on people!

"A long time I hear soldiers tell about what they do in Korea, in Vietnam. White soldiers kill yellow men—gooks! All the time I cheer inside for China, for Vietnam. The stupid white soldiers never know. They get killed over there. Good!

"That Claude! He comes to the shop in that uniform. Enemy killer of my people. Slave wife, child he steal. Big, French hero got to steal kid-bride. His money, his lies. Then he hurts her, makes her suffer. Makes her unhappy, I see. We talk, I know. I hate that Claude, long time. I want to kill him, help her. She can go home, be happy. Only it ain't easy.

"That night I play chess with Mr. Marais. I'm drunk, not too bad. He tell me Claude will come for that package. Then he gets telephone call, says I better go home. I figure it got to be Claude coming, and I see my chance. Only Mr. Marais and Claude gonna be in the shop. Mr. Marais he'll say later I left before Claude got there. My chance, you know?

"I unbolt the back door, go out the front, circle 'round to the alley and in the back way. Mr. Marais's got that package on the table, he don't hear me. I grab the iron bar to tap him a little. He hears me, starts to turn. So I jump and hit him fast. I hit too hard! He goes down. I put him in the chair, start to tie him. I see he looks funny. He's dead! I killed Mr. Marais. That Claude, it's his fault! I wait for him, but he don't come. I hear that Manet coming in the front, so I run out the back. I take the package, maybe it'll look like robbery.

"In the alley I hide. No one comes out. I hear a lot of noise inside, then the front door closes. I go to the back door again—and I hear the bell on the front door again. I look and see it's that Charlie Burgos punk. He sees Mr. Marais in the chair, runs out the front. I go in, lock the back door, and go out the front. No one sees me. I get drunk in bars, go home.

"That Manet fixed it like a robbery, I figure I'm safe. Only I'm picked up on account of the Buddha I got from Mr. Marais, and the bottle I forgot. If I tell about Manet, you know I was there after Mr. Marais was dead. You all got it wrong, only I *did* kill Mr. Marais, so I keep quiet, wait. Fortune finds the loot, and you let me go! Charlie Burgos ain't talked, so I know he's blackmailing Manet. No one will tell. I'm home free. So I get the idea—I'll use that package I got to frame Claude. Cover myself for sure, and get that Claude, too.

"I put the package in the register in the hotel when I'm visiting Li. I tell Fortune about the package, and I tip you cops. When you found the package in the register, I went into the bedroom, picked up the hat badge, said I'd found it in the register. Simple. I took the knife then, too. I got a hunch I got to kill that Burgos to frame Claude, and maybe Burgos will try to get Claude free to keep his squeeze on Manet going.

"When you let Claude out, I saw him lose your tail, but he didn't lose me. I watched him just walking around. I went and killed Burgos, left the knife. It all worked! Claude couldn't say where he was when Burgos was killed. Everyone figured Burgos seen Claude that night. No way out for Claude, and me safe.

"Then she had to do it! Li. I'm a Chinese man, a Buddhist. I got to tell the truth. She made me. I got to. For China. She die to save my karma, save me. I am a man of China, I got to tell the truth."

He sat there then in silence, erect and proud. Or was it just the release of confession? Li Marais would have said that a Buddhist could do nothing else. Marx would say that it was the same old story he had seen before—the man driven by the weight of guilt and fear to confess and find some peace. Or I could say it was the work of a sick, confused mind. Take your choice.

"Type it up," Marx said. "He signs it, then book him."

28

In the end, Viviane Marais came to my office to pay me. The next morning. She was alone. Claude Marais and Danielle didn't want to see me. I couldn't blame Claude.

"He is not bitter, Mr. Fortune," Viviane Marais said in my hot one-window office. "He says that if it had not been you, she would have found someone else. She was a normal woman, and he had driven her away."

"What will Claude do now?"

"I don't know. I doubt if he knows himself," Viviane Marais said. "Join Gerd Exner again, if Exner is freed. Find some army. Or stay and run the pawn shop for me. Who knows? Not much is solved. Except, I suppose, for Jimmy Sung. What will happen to him?"

"Bellevue first, for observation. With his background, I don't think he'll stand trial. A mental hospital, I guess."

"Is he insane, Mr. Fortune?"

"I don't know," I said. "Poor, pushed around, ignored, laughed at, a cipher among aliens. We all need identity, pride in what we are. Jimmy Sung found that in an illusion—the glory of China. Because he happened to be Chinese, but maybe more because the Chinese are the enemy today. By joining the enemy of those who despised and hurt him, being part of China in his mind, he could feel superior and despise those who ignored him. He could destroy them vicariously. He carried it too far."

"As Claude carried his rejection too far," Viviane Marais said. "He needed his illusion of the glory of France to be superior to Eugene. Then he had to reject all glory to be superior to everyone. You remember that money Claude took from his bank? It wasn't for black-mail, it was to help Gerd Exner. No matter what Exner had tried to do, he was still a lost comrade. There is still fantasy in Claude." She lit a cigarette. "Did you ever wonder why Eugene was a quiet man who did nothing, condemned no one?"

"Why?"

"Vel d'Hiv," she said, "when he did nothing. He was in love with a Jewish girl from Poland before he married me. They took her to Vel d'Hiv that night in 1942. Eugene did nothing." Viviane Marais smoked. "He would say, later, that every human being has one single moment when he learns that there is no possibility of immortality, complete-ness, or perfection. Everyone is mortal, incomplete, and imperfect. So he judged no one, looked for no glory, tried to change nothing, and had no illusions. Then he died for an illusion anyway."

She wasn't going to find it easy to accept. She wanted good rea-sons for what happened to her. That was her illusion.

"What is Danielle going to do? The police won't hold her long on the blackmail charge with Charlie Burgos dead."

"Who can say what a young girl will do?" Viviane Marais said, stood up. "Good-bye, Mr. Fortune."

She left, and ended it. Like that. Alone, I thought about Marty who was married to her director by now. Not part of this, yet a cause. If I had not needed money to try to hold Marty, I would never have taken Li Marais's job. Li might still be alive, Jimmy Sung never suspected. You never knew who or what was going to be a cause.

The tiger, or its shadow.

Jimmy Sung's desperate need for identity in a world that injured and ignored him. A need that had created an illusion that killed.

THE END

A Sneak Peek at the next Dan Fortune Mystery

**Read the first chapter
of the next exciting Dan Fortune mystery**

The Silent Scream
by Dennis Lynds
#6 in the Edgar Award-winning Dan Fortune mystery series

New York Times: "One of the year's Best Detective Novels."

We tend to dream of perfection. The perfect job, the perfect life, the perfect woman. It was a cold January day on the East Side as I came out of the subway and walked north on Lexington Avenue, and it was six months since Marty had married her director. Actress Martine Adair, my woman, but not any more. Martine Reston now. A one-armed man dreams more than most, makes perfect what never was or should have been.

She had replaced my missing arm for so long, and now in my morning mirror there was only one arm and no woman. Six months of booze, and of my watching her new apartment from a solitary doorway across the street. Finally, a morning of daylight, and the call of a client with a job. A fresh start.

So I was walking north on Lexington in the cold morning, a Wednesday, to Morgan Crafts.

It was a small store between Fifty-fifth and Fifty-sixth streets, two steps down, with only three items displayed in its window: a bright Turkish jug, a Cambodian green Buddha, and a wooden Amazonian mask. Classy. No bell tinkled as I went in. The atmosphere was hushed. More items of far-flung native crafts were displayed on shelves and in showcases. A single female clerk talked in the rear to a thin, pasty-faced man in a blue cashmere overcoat too wide and too long, as if he hoped to grow bigger.

"I'm sorry," the clerk was saying. "Mrs. Morgan is busy."

"I got to see her," the little man insisted. He tried to push past to a doorway curtained by hanging beads. The woman was bigger than he was. She blocked him.

"If you'd like to wait, or give your name," she insisted.

"Okay, I'll wait a while. Only – " The small man glanced around the shop. He saw me. His black eyes jumped in his bony face, and a livid scar twitched at the base of his long nose. He looked beyond me through the window out to the street.

"I'll come back," he said.

"If you'll tell me – " the clerk began.

Almost running, he passed me, left the door open behind him, and hurried off down Lexington.

I closed the door. "Your customers leave in a hurry." I closed the door and walked toward her.

"He wasn't a customer," she said, annoyed. "Not a normal one, anyway. He wanted to see Mrs. Morgan."

"So do I, but I have a name: Dan Fortune. Mrs. Morgan called me. Ten o'clock appointment."

She looked at a wall clock. It was five of ten.

"Well," she hesitated. "I'll see."

She pushed aside the beaded curtain and returned almost at once, smiling. Mrs. Morgan would see me. "Through the curtain, first door on the left," she told me.

I knocked on the door, a woman's voice said to come in, and I stepped into a neat, precise office. The woman sitting behind an ornate, antique desk was young. Very young. Maybe twenty-two or

-three, with big dark eyes, a full mouth in a pale-olive face, and long, straight black hair. A cool face.

"You're Mr. Fortune?" She looked me over, her face neutral but the question in her voice – a one-armed detective? It's always there.

"Private investigator," I said. "License and all."

She stood up, nodded to the man who sat quietly in a corner. An older man. His hair was white, but thick, and his swarthy, square face had a firm glow. Short and stocky, he wore a white turtle-neck and a well-cut dark blue suit. When he stood, it was an easy, fluid motion, muscular.

His voice was soft, relaxed. "Later, Mia? About four?"

"All right," Mia Morgan said.

He nodded to me and left. Mia Morgan watched then motioned me to follow her. She went into the store, stopped to say something quietly to the clerk, then continued outside in brisk strides and turned right without looking back to be sure I was behind her. She unlocked a door and climbed to the second floor, where she led me into a large, sunny apartment directly over her shop. A bohemian apartment, all bright plastic and native crafts.

"Wait here," she said.

I watched her hurry into a large bedroom with a king-sized bed under an African throw. I glanced around, saw a kitchen and a second bedroom that had been turned into a craft workshop. All the furniture and decorations were bold and individual, almost defiant.

Mia Morgan returned. She handed me a snapshot.

"I want to know who the woman in this picture is, where she lives, what she does. I want pics of the men she dates – together with her. All I know is that she frequents an East Side restaurant: Le Cerf Agile. I'll give you a week."

In the snapshot a man of average height stood with his back to the camera facing a blond woman in front of an apartment building. He wore a dark homburg, dark overcoat, and silk scarf. The blond was maybe thirty – and a beauty. A real beauty – a cover-girl face. Her blond hair curled on her shoulders from under one of those mannish felt hats Greta Garbo used to wear.

"Not much to go on," I said. "What's your interest in her?"

"You know all you need to," Mia Morgan said. "Yes or no? I can get someone else."

A detective who expected his clients to tell all wouldn't work much. A hazard of the trade. Half the time you never do learn the whole story, and Mia Morgan was right – she could get fifty other investigators who wouldn't ask questions. I needed the money, and wanted the work. I wanted to be busy. It was as good an excuse as any.

"All right," I said, looked at the apartment. "A hundred a day plus expenses. Extra for the camera work."

"Five hundred now, the rest on final bill."

I nodded. She went to a lacquered blue desk to write the check. I studied her. People who hire detectives are usually scared, angry, emotional, or nervous. She wasn't emotional, and didn't sound scared. Cold, maybe, a little tight, but not nervous. A poised, controlled girl in her early twenties who sounded and acted a lot older. Nor surprises left, as if she had been through all the youthful troubles there were and more.

She stood up with the check. "One week. Tops."

Meet the Author: Dennis Lynds

A raconteur and Renaissance man, Dennis Lynds changed the mystery form and along the way created colorful private detectives who consistently won awards as well as the hearts of readers. He was a tall, lanky man with a nose the size of Gibraltar and a generous nature that made him a soft touch for friends, panhandlers, and his children. He published some 40 novels under various pseudonyms, won awards such as the Edgar, the mystery world's highest honor, and received accolades from legendary authors like Ross Macdonald. "A novelist of power and quality, ... one of the major imaginative creators in the crime field," Macdonald wrote of him.

The New York Times named several of Lynds's novels to its Best Mysteries of the Year lists. Remarkably, two of them written under different pseudonyms appeared on the same list – *Silent Scream* by Michael Collins and *Circle of Fire* by Mark Sadler.

Amused, Lynds said that none of the *Times* editors realized he was both Collins and Sadler. "I don't think they ever figured it out," he explained. And he never bothered to tell them.

Seldom does an author change the course of a genre once; rarely twice. Lynds is credited with being the writer who, in the late 1960s and early 1970s, propelled the detective novel into the Modern Age. His most famous pen name was Michael Collins. With that name, he created the opinionated Dan Fortune, the star of one of America's longest-running private detective series. The first book, *Act of Fear*, won the Edgar Allan Poe Award for Best First Novel. "Many critics believe Dan Fortune to be the culmination of a maturing process that transformed the private eye from the naturalistic Spade (Dashiell

Hammett) through the romantic Marlowe (Raymond Chandler) and the psychological Archer (Ross Macdonald) to the sociological Fortune," according to *Private Eyes: 101 Knights* by Robert Baker and Michael Nietzel.

At heart, Lynds was a rebel. Two decades later, he rattled mystery critics and changed the field again, this time by introducing literary techniques into the genre, beginning in the late 1980s with *Red Rosa, Castrato*, and *Chasing Eights*, and continuing well into the 1990s with *The Irishman's Horse, Cassandra in Red*, and *The Cadillac Cowboy*. Other authors followed, proving the flexibility and durability of the suspense world. "No one could accuse [Lynds] of reworking the same turf in his novels. ... His last several books have pushed the private-eye form into some fascinating new shapes," according to *The Wall Street Journal* in 2000. *The Los Angeles Times* commented, "It takes style to bring that off. Bravery, too, of course."

Lynds also published mainstream novels, short stories, and poetry. Five of his literary short stories were honored in *Best American Short Stories*.

During World War II, he was a rifleman and carried books of poetry in his knapsack as he fought across France. He was a strong swimmer, so when he and fellow infantrymen were surrounded by Nazis, he plunged into an icy river, leading them to escape. He earned two Purple Hearts and a Bronze Star. Later he graduated with a degree in chemistry from Hofstra and a masters degree in journalism from Syracuse. A lifelong New Yorker, in the mid 1960s he finally left the East Coast's bitter winters to settle in the warm sunshine of Southern California. He was married three times, to Doris Flood, then Sheila McErlean, and finally to Gayle Hallenbeck Stone Lynds. He had two daughters, Katie and Deirdre Lynds, and two step children, Paul and Julia Stone.

Dennis Lynds died at age 81 in 2005. Jack Adrian wrote in *The Financial Times*, "Unusually for a mystery writer – as a breed, they tend to favor things as they are, rather than as they might be – the American author Dennis Lynds, politically, came from left of center.

This did not mean he preached bloody revolution. He wrote to entertain." Entertainment was something Lynds never forgot, that and to be generous to his friends.

Obituaries celebrating his work appeared around the globe. In a typical understatement, he commented near the end of his life, "I had a good run." His career had lasted more than fifty years.

The Back Cover

Shadow of a Tiger
#5 in the Edgar Award–winning Dan Fortune mystery series
by Dennis Lynds
Originally published under the pseudonym Michael Collins

It's summer in New York, 1972, and the city is steaming. Actress Martine Adair can't stand it any longer. She sends her lover off to pawn the diamond ring he gave her, so they can spend the next month cooling off at the beach. Her lover is private detective Dan Fortune, who works the dangerous alleys and high rises of the edgy Chelsea district.

At the neighborhood pawnshop, Fortune not only picks up cash, he meets Claude Marais and his wife. Claude is a retired soldier who fought on the losing side during France's humiliating defeats at Dien Bien Phu and Algiers. Convinced someone is trying to kill him, Claude's wife asks Fortune to stand guard outside their hotel room that night. Fortune agrees – the money will be enough to redeem Marty's ring and still take her to the beach.

In the morning Claude is fine, but his brother – Fortune's friend, the gentle pawnbroker – is dead, his skull bashed in. The police think it's a robbery gone bad, but Fortune disagrees – why would a robber leave $300 untouched in the cash drawer, and besides, how could the thief have gotten into the highly secure shop, unless the pawnbroker himself let him in? It had to be an inside job, yet the pawnbroker apparently had no enemies, no dark secrets.

Foreign adventurers, vicious gang members, an exotic beauty from Thailand, and an alcoholic Chinese man populate this riveting tale, leading Fortune to a hair-raising ending and revelations of a tortured past no one wanted to remember but few could let die.

New York Times: "One of the year's Best Mysteries."

"First-class ... suspenseful, character-rich, and absorbing." – *Kirkus Reviews*

"Some of the rawest, most unencumbered mystery writing extant in the genre." – *American Library Association*

"Subtle undercurrents, handled with perception and realism ... a logical conclusion of force and stunning power." – *Utica Observer-Dispatch*

"[Lynds's books are] filled with as much closely observed incident and detail as John O'Hara's short stories ..." – *Wall Street Journal*

###